Mildred
Pierced

ALSO BY STUART M. KAMINSKY

MILDRED PIERCED

A TOBY PETERS MYSTERY

STUART M. KAMINSKY

An Otto Penzler Book

———

CARROLL & GRAF PUBLISHERS
NEW YORK

MILDRED PIERCED
A TOBY PETERS MYSTERY

Carroll & Graf Publishers
An Otto Penzler Book
An Imprint of Avalon Publishing Group Inc.
161 William Street, 16th Floor
New York, NY 10038

Copyright © 2003 by Stuart M. Kaminsky

First Carroll & Graf cloth edition 2003

Library of Congress Cataloging-in-Publication Data is available.

ISBN: 0-7867-1182-5

Printed in the United States of America
Distributed by Publishers Group West

And this one is for
the one and only Annie Miller

"Why so disheartened!" he exclaimed. "The scoundrel must be concealed behind some of these trees, and may yet be secured. We are not safe while he goes at large."

—James Fenimore Cooper,
The Last of the Mohicans

CHAPTER

1

UNTIL WEDNESDAY AFTERNOON January 5, 1944, there had been no deaths, intentional or accidental, caused by the firing of a crossbow in the recorded history of Los Angeles County.

On that day, while the German army of Field Marshal Fritz von Manstein was retreating into the Pripet marshes in Poland and the U.S. Marines were driving the Japanese back at Cape Gloucester in New Britain in the Pacific, Mildred Binder Minck made history.

The day after Mildred's historic demise, I sat across from her grieving widower, Sheldon Minck, D.D.S., in a room in the Los Angeles County Jail.

The Los Angeles County Hall of Justice on Temple Street between Broadway and Spring takes up a city block. It's fourteen stories of limestone and granite, an Italian Renaissance style building with rusticated stonework, heavy cornices, and a two-story colonnade at the top.

The L.A. County Jail occupies the five top stories. Sheldon

1

Minck, D.D.S., was occupying only one chair on the fourth floor of the jail. He faced me through a wall of thick wire mesh.

"Toby, I didn't do it," he said.

Shelly Minck is not a thing of beauty to behold when he's at his best, happily drilling into or removing the tooth of a trapped patient. Seated on the other side of the wire, he was not at his best.

"I mean, I don't think I did it," he added.

Shelly wore a pair of dark slacks and a long-sleeved wrinkled gray shirt. His thick glasses rested, as they usually did, at the end of his ample nose. Beads of sweat danced on his bald head and his large stomach heaved with frequent sighs.

"They won't let me have a cigar," he complained. "Is that fair?"

I didn't answer. He squinted around the room. Along either side of the mesh wall were chairs facing each other, twelve chairs, and a narrow wooden shelf on either side so prisoners could drum their fingers, fold their hands, or examine their bitten nails. On the other side, lawyers could take notes or safely give their clients bad news.

There was only one other prisoner with a visitor. He was a thin man with wild hair who needed a shave. His visitor was an even thinner woman with even more wild hair, who needed to decide which of the three colors that roamed through that hair was the one she planned to live with.

It was early in the morning, and each newly arrested inmate was allowed a morning visitor the day after his arrest.

"You should have called Marty Leib," I said.

Marty Leib was a criminal defense attorney whom I called when I needed legal rescue. As a licensed private investigator, I needed rescue more often than I could afford so I saved his services for emergencies. Marty was good, expensive, immoral. He wore fine clothes, weighed about three hundred pounds, and always seemed happy to hear from me and start the fee clock ticking.

"You call him for me. It's you I need. You find criminals," said Shelly.

"I conduct investigations for paying clients," I said.

Shelly looked hurt. Shelly looked as if he were going to weep. I cut him off.

"Okay, I'll call Marty."

"And you'll help me?"

I sublet a small office off of Sheldon Minck's dental chamber of horrors in the Farraday Building downtown. The office was not soundproof. I knew when Shelly had a patient. I could hear the drill, the screams and Shelly's soothing voice either singing or trying to calm the hysterical patient with his singing. Shelly thought he sounded like Nelson Eddy. On one of his better days, I thought he approached Andy Devine.

"I'll see what I can do," I said.

He looked at his hands. His glasses almost fell off. He pushed them back.

"Why would I kill Mildred?"

I could come up with four good reasons. Mildred had not long ago thrown Shelly out of their house, cleaned out their joint bank account, taken in a slightly overage stuntman, and filed for divorce demanding half of everything Shelly would make for the rest of his life.

Since Mildred had thrown him out, Shelly had been living in a very small hotel room.

"She had a few faults, but I loved her, Toby," he said with less-than-attractive but probably sincere emotion.

I believed him, though I had no idea why he had blinded himself to Mildred's "few faults." Mildred was skinny, homely, harping, and unfaithful. She belittled Shelly in front of other people and made it clear that any pal of his was probably not worth space on the planet. I stood at the top of Mildred's list of the unworthy.

3

"I know, Shel," I said. "What were you doing in Lincoln Park at eleven in the morning with a crossbow?"

"Shooting it," he explained.

I nodded.

"Not at Mildred," he added quickly. "I set up a target. I didn't know Mildred was there. I don't know what she was doing there. I didn't even see her till she fell. "

"You've got a great defense, Shelly," I said. "You couldn't see what you were shooting at, missed the target, and hit your wife who you didn't know was there. Did you have your glasses off?"

"No," he insisted loudly enough that the skinny prisoner and his visitor five chairs down to his right turned to look our way. "I didn't take my glasses off. Well, I did, but that was before I fired. I wiped the sweat from my eyes."

"Are you an expert with a crossbow, Shel?"

"No, I've only fired it five times. I'm getting better, but I think I'll give it up now."

"Might be a good idea," I said. "Why a crossbow?"

"I've joined Lawrence Timerjack's Survivors for the Future," he said. "We learn how to make our own weapons and use them, forage for food, hide from the enemy and survive. I'm a Pigeon now. When I complete the training, I become a Pathfinder."

I needed a cup of coffee.

"You see," Shelly said, leaning forward. "Our bible is the complete works of the first great American novelist, James Fenimore Cooper, who devoted his life to writing about surviving on the frontier."

"And killing Indians," I said.

"That, too," he agreed. "Pigeons are the lowest level. Pigeon is the Delaware nickname for the young Natty Bumppo."

"Who?"

"Natty Bumppo," he said with enthusiasm. "He went from being called the Pathfinder, to Deerslayer and then—"

"Why?" I asked.

"Why what?"

"Why do you want to become a Survivor for the Future?"

"In case America is overrun by the Asian hordes, or the Arabs or Nazis or creatures from another planet or the government goes nuts. It could happen."

"We're winning the war, Shel," I tried. "It's almost over."

He shook his head at my naïveté.

"This time," he said. "But the next time? What if we have to move to Australia or some jungle somewhere or a desert?"

"Where do the Survivors for the Future hang around?"

"We don't hang around," he said, mustering a healthy touch of indignation as he adjusted his glasses again. "We have a campsite and cabins on Hollywood Lake. It's secluded, rustic, wooded, the ideal place—"

"Let's try something else," I interrupted. "If you didn't kill Mildred, who did?"

"I don't know. I was standing straight, both eyes open, focused, bow pulled back, bolt in place. Concentrating, you know?"

"Bolt?"

"Crossbows shoot bolts or quarrels or arrows," he explained. "Depends on where they're made. A bolt is . . . well, a bolt of metal, sort of shaped like a pointy pencil with a kind of tail, all one piece of metal."

"How many of these bolts had you fired yesterday before . . . "

"None," Shelly said, holding up a single finger. "That was the first. I had three bolts with me. The police took the other two. The ones I didn't shoot."

Shelly looked dreamily past my right shoulder. I turned to see what he was looking at. It was a painting of Indians greeting Spanish conquistadors on the Pacific coast. The Indians were holding out baskets of food. The Spanish, in full armor, were holding out what looked like orange blankets. The Indians were wearing tomahawks on their hips. The Spaniards were wearing swords. There wasn't a crossbow in sight.

"Shelly?"

"Huh?"

"In the park. Crossbow. You pulled the string or whatever it's called back and then . . . "

"I fired," he said.

Silence while he shook his head and then focused, slightly open-mouthed, on something behind me.

"Shelly."

"Huh?"

"I need you here in Los Angeles," I said. "Not in the woods with the Deerfinder."

He sighed deeply. "Deer*slayer.* I looked up and there was Mildred, lying there ten feet from the target. I dropped the cross-bow and ran to her. She was dead, Toby, dead, a hole in her chest. I looked around for help and there was this woman standing there, back where I'd shot from. She was holding a paper bag."

"She saw what happened?"

"I guess," he said. "No, she must have, but she started to run. I called to her and tried to get up to go after her, but she was gone."

"And then. . . ?"

"A kid came. Asked me what was wrong. I told him my wife was hurt, that I thought she had a heart attack. He looked at Mildred and said he saw blood."

"And you—"

"I think I closed my eyes and cried. When I opened them, the kid was gone."

He shrugged.

"What did the kid look like?"

"Skinny, reddish hair, maybe fifteen, sixteen."

"That's when the police came?"

He hesitated, looked as if he were going to say something, and then simply nodded.

"She was with the two policemen," he said. "The woman with the paper bag. She was pointing to me and saying she saw me do it. That's when I recognized her."

"Who is she?"

"Joan Crawford," he said.

"You mean someone who *looks* like Joan Crawford."

"I guess." He shook his head again. "This woman was shorter than Crawford and she's got regular shoulders. And she told the police her name was Billie Castle or something like that."

The skinny couple five or six chairs down had their faces almost against the mesh now, whispering. Maybe she was going to slip him a wire cutter. Shelly and I both looked at them.

"I'm forlorn," Shelly said, looking back at me with as insincere a look of woe as I had ever seen from him, and I had seen many.

"I'll call Marty Leib," I said.

"And you'll find out who killed Mildred?" he asked as I got up.

"I'll do what I can."

"I can pay. Now that Mildred's dead, I'll get the house back, and I won't have to give her any more money."

There was no point in telling him not to pass that information on to the police. They would find it out on their own.

"You work out payment with Marty," I said. "I'll just charge you expenses."

"You're a friend," Shelly said with the sincerity of a bad child actor. "And Toby . . . "

"Yes, Shel."

"When you come back, bring me some cigars, nothing expensive. I've got to have them. It's like life or death."

I nodded. Life or death might well be involved here, but it wasn't about cigars.

"I'll see what I can do," I said.

I didn't look back at him when the guard let me out of the room. In the hall waiting for the elevator, I pulled out my notebook, crumpled, wire, spirals bent, found the blunt pencil in my pocket and wrote three names: Joan Crawford?, Lawrence Timerjack, and Phil Pevsner. There was a question mark after the name of Joan Crawford because I knew that Crawford had once used the name Billie Cassin, and that she was born with the unlikely name Lucille Fay Le Sueur. I knew because I had worked at Warner Brothers as a security guard and had plenty of time to read the fan magazines, even though it was considered an act of treachery by the Brothers Warner to read about MGM stars like Crawford.

Phil Pevsner is my brother, a lieutenant in the Los Angeles Police Department. He works out of the Wilshire Station. I was born Tobias Leo Pevsner and changed my name to Toby Peters when I became a cop. That was before my Warner Brothers days. My brother had never forgiven me for the name change, but then again, there was a long list of things for which he had never forgiven me and a short list for things for which he *had* forgiven me. I was working on making the long list shorter, which wasn't always easy given his temper and my inability to keep from making him mad.

I headed for my brother.

When I found a parking space for my Crosley, I checked the grocery list in my pocket. I was supposed to pick up what was on the list for my landlady, Mrs. Plaut. Irene Plaut was ancient and determined. Neither ration stamps nor common sense got in her way, and when one of the tenants in her boardinghouse tried to employ logic, her hearing aid conveniently failed.

The Ration Board allotted each American forty-eight points a month and warned us not to use them all up during the first week.

I was to pick up a pound of bacon (no more than thirty-nine cents), a pound of oleo (no more than seventeen cents), a No. 2 can of green beans (for eleven cents), and two pounds of sirloin steak at forty-two cents a pound. The tenants had all chipped in their ration coupons, and Mrs. Plaut had given me exactly enough cash.

When she had caught me hurrying down the stairs that morning, heading for the door and my meeting with Sheldon Minck, she had handed me the list, instructions, coupons. She grabbed my arm. She weighs about as much as a sponge cake and stands no more than four-feet-eight, but she has the grip of a Swedish plumber.

"Breakfast," she had said.

"No time," I answered. "Dr. Minck is in trouble."

"Then he should see an eye doctor," she said. "Not an exterminator."

Mrs. Plaut is actually under the dual delusion that I am not only an exterminator, but also a book editor. Both fantasies had been gleaned from bits of conversation which then were cemented in her mind as undeniable truth. Thus, one of my duties as a tenant in the House of Plaut on Heliotrope Street was to read chapters of the ongoing family history she was writing.

"An eye doctor?" I asked before I could stop myself.

"That's what the mister did when he was seeing double before the big war—not this one, but the *big* one."

"He's in trouble," I had semi-shouted, "not seeing double."

"Bugs?"

"What?" I said, wondering where this was going.

"He has bugs?"

"Yes," I said.

"Unsanitary," she said with disapproval. "I've given my bird a new name."

"Great," I said, trying to escape.

Mrs. Plaut was constantly changing the name of her squawking bird, which either sat asleep on the perch in its cage or went wild. Mrs. Plaut's rooms were right off the front door at the bottom of the stairs. The door was open.

Getting past her was a challenge I rarely met. The bird was quiet.

"I have renamed him Jamaica Red," she said.

The bird was brown and green, some kind of little parrot. I doubted if it came from Jamaica.

"Great name," I said.

She smiled.

"He seems to like it. It soothes his savage breast."

With that, she had let go of my arm and I fled.

The Crosley didn't use much gas, which was good because there was a major gas shortage. It didn't matter if you had the coupons or not. There just wasn't much gas, which suddenly made my tiny automobile a valuable means of transportation. No-Neck Arnie the mechanic had offered me what I had bought it from him for plus forty dollars. I had turned him down. It wasn't easy getting in and out of, but it was easy to park and seemed to run on the memory of gasoline.

There were four people waiting on a wooden bench in the lobby facing the uniformed desk clerk at the Wilshire Street Station, a warhorse named Corso whom I knew would be ready for pasture in less than a year.

"Toby," he called out. "How's it going?"

"I'm blessed with beauty, wealth, and a heart full of fellowship," I said. "Life is wonderful."

Corso shook his head and laughed, but it sounded more like a grunt.

It didn't take much to make him laugh. He had been born with the looks of a bewildered bull. I was a flat-nosed former cop pushing fifty who looked more like a backup thug in a gangster picture than a leading man. I lived from client to client and sometimes kept from getting behind on my rent by filling in for a vacationing or sick house detective in one of the downtown hotels.

I started for the stairs when he waved me back.

"She's in the hospital again," Corso said softly, looking at the family of four sitting on the bench patiently to be sure they weren't listening.

"She" was my brother Phil's wife, Ruth, the mother of my two nephews, Nathan and David, and my four-year-old niece, Lucy. Ruth had been sick for almost two years, in and out of the hospital, almost not making it out the last two times. I had been at their house two Sundays ago. There was almost nothing left of Ruth, yet she had made dinner and tried to pay attention to the conversation. We had listened to *The Aldrich Family*, or pretended to.

"How bad?" I asked.

Corso shrugged.

"Don't know. Can't be good. Thought you should know before you went up to see him. You know?"

I knew. Phil didn't accept frustration, which was most of the reason he had been reduced from captain to lieutenant a little over a year earlier. Death was an enemy. Every criminal on both sides of the prison walls was an enemy. When I wasn't being careful, I was a convenient focus for his rage. He wasn't going gently into that good night, and he wouldn't let anyone else, either.

"I'll be careful," I told Corso and tapped my palm on his desk.

"Just thought you should know," he said.

I nodded and went up the wooden stairs to the landing and into the squad room. It was a quiet morning. There were nine desks in the space designed for six desks. Along the door by the wall was a wooden bench. No one was sitting on it. Four of the desks had cops behind them. Two were typing reports. Two were talking to victims, witnesses, or suspects. It was hard to tell since both of the people in the chairs next to the desks were young Mexicans who looked decidedly unhappy. The rest of the cops were probably out on the street.

The squad room didn't smell or look as bad as it usually did. The walls hadn't been cleaned, but the floor was relatively free of crumpled paper, cigarette packs, and candy wrappers. The windows seemed to be letting in a little more light, but not enough.

I crossed the room behind the desks and knocked at the door of my brother's office. No answer. I knocked again. No answer. I opened the door.

Phil's office was about twice the size of mine, which meant his office was small. It looked as if a Benedictine monk had furnished it. Two chairs. A desk. One window behind the desk. Nothing on the walls. The office of a man who could empty his drawers into a box and be moved out in two minutes or less.

Phil sat behind the desk, his back to me, hands behind his head looking out of the window at nothing.

"Did I say 'come in'?" he said evenly. Definitely a bad sign.

"No."

I left it at that. He sighed, rubbed the military-style short gray hair on his head and swiveled toward me. He was twenty pounds heavier than I was, five years older, and made up in weary hardness what he lacked in homeliness.

He was wearing suspenders today over a white shirt. He folded his hands on the desk and looked up at me.

"Sit down," he said.

I sat. I said nothing. He said nothing. He didn't seem to be in a hurry. This was a tranquil Phil I had never seen before. I didn't like it. I didn't trust it.

"Can I take you out for lunch?" I asked.

"Too early. Not hungry."

"Can I get you a coffee?"

"You know about Ruth?" he said.

"Yeah."

"I'm taking some time off to be with her." He looked down at his hands. "She hasn't got long."

"I'm sorry."

"I know. You didn't come to ask about Ruth."

"No."

"You came about Minck."

I nodded.

"Not my case. Not in the district," he said. "I *did* ask to look at the report."

"And?"

He reached over to the six-inch pile of files and memos in his IN box, took a single sheet from the top, and laid it in front of him.

"He's a lunatic, Tobias."

"I know."

"No," Phil said again. "A lunatic. In the park with a goddamn crossbow? We could put him away for that. He's half blind and all stupid. Shoots his wife with an arrow on a sunny day with a witness."

"Bolt," I said. "Not an arrow, a bolt. Crossbows fire bolts, quarrels . . ."

"Who gives a shit?" Phil said. "He killed her. He can plead insanity. You're getting Leib for him?"

"Yes."

"Any judge in his right mind will buy insanity after talking to Minck for five minutes, especially with Leib next to him," said Phil. "Ballistics is looking at the bow and the piece of metal that killed her. They don't know what to do with it. I could tell them where they could put that . . ."

"Bolt," I supplied. "Where did it hit her?"

"Perfect shot," said Phil. "Right in the heart."

"How far away was he?"

"Witness says about twenty yards."

"Phil, can you imagine Shelly firing anything including a cannon and hitting a target twenty yards away?"

"I can imagine almost anything," he said. "I can imagine a lucky shot or an unlucky one. If insanity doesn't work, he can claim it was an accident. He doesn't look like Robin Hood. He doesn't even look like the fat guy who played Friar Tuck."

"Eugene Pallette," I said.

"I'll remember that."

"He didn't do it, Phil," I said.

"You're sure?"

"No," I said. "But I'm staying with it till I am sure."

"Good luck," he said.

"How are you holding up?"

"How do I look?"

"I've seen you better. I've seen you worse."

"The commissioner's seeing me this afternoon," he said, turning his head away to look at a blank wall.

"What happened?"

He didn't answer, so I guessed, "You hit a suspect."

"I beat the hell out of the bastard," Phil said. "Shoot-out last night at the playground on Ocean View. Two guys with guns, a grudge over a woman with practically no teeth, their guts full of cheap wine. One of them, Herman Winterhoff, accidentally shot an eleven-year-old girl minding her own business. The officers who took the call brought him in for interrogation. When I got to Winterhoff, the bastard was smiling at me. He wasn't smiling when I left the room."

"Witnesses?"

"Cawelti, Minor, Harell."

"They'll back you."

"Not Cawelti," he said.

He was right. The redheaded, pockmarked detective John Cawelti was not going to be part of the blue wall of silence for Phil, whom he hated only a little less than Cawelti hated me. Cawelti was probably picturing himself in this luxury office.

"You'll be all right," I said. "You've got a lot on your mind. The commissioner will—"

"Not this time." Phil turned his back to me again.

"Phil?"

He didn't answer. I didn't try again. I got up and went to the door. I thought of saying "Good luck" or "I'll call about Ruth" or something, but Phil was lost in whatever world he was trying to hide in.

There had been one witness to Mildred's death. It was time to see her.

CHAPTER

I KNEW WHERE Joan Crawford's house was in Brentwood. That wasn't hard to find. Getting her to talk to me would be the hard part, so I called in a favor from Fred Astaire who knew her. I had recently worked for and with him to get him out of a bad situation. I liked Astaire and he liked me, enough to make a call to Crawford.

Until the war, movie stars had been indentured—and usually well paid—by studios which, when the price was right, loaned them to other studios. Astaire had been with RKO. Crawford, until she walked out or was pushed out of her contract two years earlier, had been with MGM. Most of the people I knew in the business had been with or still were with Warner Brothers. I had spent five years there as a security guard until the day I punched a B-movie cowboy star who had been making a young actress more than uncomfortable on the set. I broke his nose. They had to shoot the movie he was making around him. I had the distinction of being fired directly by Harry Warner.

I knew a little about Crawford, the things that everyone—fans and movie people—knew, and some things only a few people knew. For example, everyone knew that she had been married to Douglas Fairbanks, Jr. and Franchot Tone and was now married to Phillip Terry, whose movie career had taken a dive into the La Brea Tar Pits.

Crawford had been linked romantically to almost every male star she had ever acted with, which made the list stretch all the way back to Lon Chaney, Sr., in the silent days, and on up to Robert Montgomery and Clark Gable in the more recent past.

Crawford also had the reputation of being unpredictable. Thirty-nine years old the morning I rang her bell, she was reportedly supportive of younger actors. Actresses her own age or close to it, however, could expect no mercy.

The world knew she had two young adopted children, Christina and Phillip, Jr. The world did not know, but Astaire told me, that she was "unusually interested in cleanliness."

"Every time she gets a new husband, she changes the toilet seats," he said on the phone. "She . . . you'll see. She's an underrated actress, and an underrated dancer. I worked with her in my first picture. Never got the chance again, but she was generous, rehearsed hard. I'd be happy to be in a picture with her again. I'll give her a call."

My pants were tan and reasonably clean if a bit frayed at the bottom should someone look closely. My shirt was white and not too badly wrinkled. My tie was simple, dark brown, and showed none of the stains I knew had to be there.

Before I rang the doorbell, I looked at my reflection in the small window at eye level. I'm not sure I'd open the door for the face I saw: My nose is almost flat, and some of the scar tissue shows if you look closely. I have a lopsided grin that looks more like a threat than a smile. I brushed back my dark hair, which revealed more than a little gray and tried not to smile.

I rang again.

She opened the door. I recognized the face. It was definitely Joan Crawford, shorter than I imagined her, about five-four, softer looking without makeup. She was wearing a blue-and-white bandanna around her hair and was dressed in slacks and a dark shirt, covered by a green-stained white apron. She wore heavy gloves and carried a pointed trowel in her right hand.

"You're . . . ?" She examined me.

"Toby Peters," I said. "Fred Astaire said he was going to call you about me."

"He did. Come in, but take off your shoes and leave them in the hallway."

She stepped back as I knelt to remove my shoes.

"Your hands," she said.

I looked up.

"Show me your hands, please," she said with a smile that pleaded for indulgence.

I showed her my hands.

"I'd appreciate it if you would wash your hands. I'll show you where."

I finished with my shoes and placed them just inside the door. She closed it and led the way.

"We use only half the house now," she said.

I wondered if the reason was that she hadn't made a movie in over two years except for a walk-on as herself in *Hollywood Canteen* or because her husband Phil Terry's career had gone from almost up there to out of the business.

She led the way to a small, sunshine-bright kitchen, then turned to smile at me as she nodded toward the sink.

"I was working in the garden," she said proudly, looking at the window.

I looked out it myself as I washed. There was a good-sized vegetable garden. She put down the trowel, took off her gloves, and laid them all neatly on a table near the back door.

"Nice," I said, rinsing my hands and looking for a towel.

"Thank you. To your right, on the rack."

There were two clean white hand towels. I dried my hands and started to put the towel back.

"No," she said sharply. "Under the sink. There's a bin for used towels."

I opened the door under the sink, found the bin, and dropped the towel in. Then I turned. Dr. Peters was ready for surgery. I felt like holding up my hands and waiting for her to put rubber gloves on me the way the nurses did for Lew Ayres in the Dr. Kildare movies.

"This way," she said, turning and walking out of the kitchen into the dining room.

"Please," she said pleasantly. "Have a seat."

I sat. So did she. She pulled an unopened pack of cigarettes from her apron, opened it, lit one, and pulled a clean ashtray toward her from the center of the table.

"I'm sorry," she said. "Would you like some coffee?"

I felt like asking if she planned to throw the cup away after I drank from it, but settled for a simple "No, thanks."

"Fred said you are an honest man and that you have some questions for me," she said. "I have one for you. Ask your questions. Then I'll ask mine."

"Okay," I said. "This is about the woman you saw killed in Lincoln Park yesterday."

She looked at the ceiling and sighed. "So everyone knows. I was afraid of that."

"Everyone *doesn't* know. You gave the name 'Billie Cassin' when you were interviewed by the police," I said. "But Shelly Minck recognized you, or thinks he did."

"Shelly. . . ?"

"The fat little man in the park with the crossbow. Your real name is not on the report."

"Not yet." She shook her head. "Cassin was my stepfather's name. I was called Billie when I was a young girl. I didn't even know it wasn't my real name."

"Can you tell me what you saw yesterday?" I asked. "I know you told the police. I read the report, but they've already decided they have their killer."

"The funny-looking little bald-headed fat man with the thick glasses?" she asked.

I nodded.

"Why are you. . . ?"

"Sheldon Minck is a dentist. I share office space with him."

"Fred said you're a private investigator."

She was smoking nervously now.

"I sublet an office from Shelly," I said. "I've known him a long time. I can't see him committing a murder."

"It was his wife, I understand?"

"Mildred," I said.

"That's a coincidence," she said.

"Coincidence?"

"I've just been offered the lead in a movie called *Mildred Pierce*. Wonderful script. It's about a woman who confesses to killing her philandering husband."

"Did she do it?"

Crawford laughed.

"See the movie when it comes out," she said.

"Mildred Minck was a philanderer, too," I said.

Crawford looked serious now. "That doesn't help your dentist."

"I know. Mildred was no great beauty and not much in the way of charm, either. But she was determined."

"All right." She put out what was left of her cigarette and folded her hands on the table. "Yesterday. About eleven in the morning. I was going to meet Phil, my husband, for an early lunch."

"Where?"

"I had it with me in a paper bag," she said. "He was getting off work at the airplane factory in order to try out for a part in a film. Mr. Peters, it wouldn't be difficult for you to find out my husband is working in an airplane factory while his agent tries to find him roles. We have no servants. We use only half the house to keep expenses down. I make his lunch and dinner and take care of the house and children. They are out this afternoon at a birthday party."

My look must have given away something about what I was thinking.

"Yes, Joan Crawford is, at the moment, only a housewife. But that is about to change."

"*Mildred Pierce?*"

"Exactly," she said. "And I don't want morbid headlines that might make the studio change its small collective mind about the movie. *Joan Crawford Eyewitness to Bizarre Murder. Dentist Murders Wife in Front of Joan Crawford. Movie Star Watches While Man Murders Wife.* You understand?"

"And . . . ?"

"I think I'd like to ask my questions now." She leaned toward me, her eyes sincere and just a little moist. "I would like to hire you to keep my name out of the press. I understand from Fred and I've heard from several other friends in the business that you specialize in doing just that. So. . . ?"

"I'm investigating the murder of Mildred Minck," I said. "I'm working for Dr. Minck."

"Are the tasks mutually exclusive?" she asked, her eyes open wide.

She didn't blink. Movie stars don't blink when the camera is on them and they're doing a take. Crawford was doing a take.

"No," I said. "I don't think so."

"Good." She sat back and reached into her pocket for her now-open pack of cigarettes. "Shall I consider you hired?"

"Don't you want to know my rates?"

"I'm not working," she said. "But I'm not penniless, either. I've made quite a bit over the past twenty years."

"Thirty dollars a day plus expenses," I said. "Two hundred dollar retainer, nonrefundable, not applicable to the total."

"That sounds reasonable," she said. "I hope you don't mind cash. I'd rather not have any canceled checks made out to a private investigator."

"Cash is fine."

"Wait."

I sat waiting. This wasn't what I expected. I hadn't even asked her about the "alleged" murder yet. I'd learned to use the word "alleged" from Marty Leib. There was always hope that the crime, if I was representing the accused, was an accident—or the work of someone else.

I reached over for the pack of cigarettes she had left on the table and started turning it over and over just to keep my fingers busy. I don't smoke. Never did. Neither did my brother or our father.

I was still playing with the pack when she returned. She stopped suddenly, the cash in her hand, and watched me. Then she handed me the bills, reached over and took the pack, and walked into the kitchen. I turned to watch her through the open door as she stepped on the pedal of a tan metal trash can and dropped the cigarette pack into it. The lid dropped down. She returned to the dinning room and sat across from me reaching into her pocket for a fresh pack.

"You'll give me an itemized bill when you're finished."

"Yes."

"If you succeed in keeping my name from the press"—she opened the fresh pack and gave me a look that said don't-touch-this-one-or-you'll-be-sorry—"I'll give you a bonus of three hundred dollars."

"Very generous," I said.

"I believe in incentives," she said. "Now. You want to know what I saw. . . . "

I put the bills she had given me into my pants pocket without looking at them.

"It's very simple," she said, removing the cellophane from the pack in her hand. "It was near the tennis courts."

"Was there anyone playing?"

"No. I came down the path behind a patch of trees."

"And you saw no one?"

"On the path? No."

"Don't people recognize you?" I asked.

"I was wearing dark glasses and a wide-brimmed hat and a plain dress with very little makeup. Most people seem to think I'm just a housewife who bears a slight resemblance to Joan Crawford."

I thought, but didn't say, that in Los Angeles nothing calls more attention to someone than dark glasses and a wide-brimmed hat.

"He was standing there," she said. "With that thing out of an old costume drama."

"The crossbow," I supplied.

"I saw the woman start to take her hand out of her purse and go to her knees and fall backward," Crawford went on, looking at the backs of her hands.

"How close was she to the target?"

She shrugged. "About fifteen feet or so to the right of it."

"You saw him fire the crossbow?"

"Yes."

"And then she went down?"

"Yes."

"He was aiming it at her?"

"I don't know. He was waving it around before he pulled the

23

trigger or did whatever one does to fire. I was looking only because it seemed so odd to see someone in the middle of the lawn with such a weapon."

"How did he react when he saw her go down?"

Crawford looked up, a slightly puzzled expression on her face.

"Peculiarly," she said. "For an instant, he didn't react at all, just looked in the general direction of the target and then it was evident that he saw the woman falling. He looked . . . "

"Surprised?" I supplied.

"Surprised, stunned, horrified by what he had done. Certainly not calm and composed. He went over to her and knelt. I hurried back down the path. I found a policeman about five minutes away and told him what had happened."

"You didn't see anyone on the path? A skinny redheaded kid?"

"Oh, yes. On a bicycle. He drove past me just before I saw the policeman. I don't think I told the police about the boy. Is it important?"

"The boy stopped to help Shelly. Shelly says he told the kid he thought his wife had a heart attack," I said.

"I'm not sure that proves—" she began.

"—that Shelly didn't know his wife had been shot," I finished.

"If he was telling the boy the truth, and he didn't kill his wife. . . ." She smiled.

"Then you didn't see him kill her and you're out of it," I said.

Her smile disappeared.

"But I *did* see him shoot her."

"We'll get back to that. What happened after you got the policeman?"

"I waited for the officer on a bench near where I had found him. He ran down the path toward the lawn where I had pointed. And that's all."

"Would you mind showing me in the park where all this took place?"

"Can it wait till tomorrow morning? I have to pick up the children, and Phillip is coming home early."

She looked at me earnestly. If she had been convinced my hands were clean, I think she would have touched me.

"What time did you see Mildred Minck get killed? I mean, was it right at eleven?"

"A few minutes past," she said.

There wasn't anything more to ask. We decided that I would pick her up at nine the next morning after the children were in school and her husband was at work. I wanted to look at the scene at the same time and, if possible, in the same light as when Mildred had died.

We walked back to the front door, passing a large living room with thin metallic lamps and sofas that looked never sat upon.

She stood in the doorway while I walked toward my car. I turned to watch her. She was wearing a sad, put-upon smile.

London could take it. The smile said Joan Crawford could, too.

It was late in the afternoon. I decided to find Lawrence Timerjack, founder of Shelly's Survivors for the Future.

CHAPTER

3

I DROVE UP Cahuenga Boulevard toward the Hollywood Hills and turned right onto Holly Drive. From there it was a series of about twelve turns onto small, winding streets. I got lost, had to turn around and asked a pair of ten-year-olds how to get to Hollywood Lake.

It took me five more minutes to hit Hollywood Lake and another ten to find a low fence that surrounded three log cabins about fifty yards away from the lake shore.

The gate in the fence was simply a thin log with a wooden sign next to it with the words "Survivors for the Future: Just wait. We'll see you."

I parked and stood in front of the gate, pretending to admire the woods on either side of the fenced property that seemed to be about the size of a small city block.

I could have simply lifted the log and walked in or climbed over the fence. The place was not really built for survival in case of enemy attack.

After about three minutes, the door to the middle cabin opened and four people came out. The one in the lead was small and wiry. He had short-cropped blond hair and was wearing a black short-sleeved pullover T-shirt and denim slacks tucked into army boots. He held a bow in his right hand and a quiver of arrows bounced on his back.

Following him were a man, a boy, and a woman.

The boy was about seventeen, the woman in her forties. The fellow with them was steel-gray-haired, bronzed, with a craggy face, and around fifty. He had a holster and gun strapped under his left arm. They were all dressed like the man they were following. As they came closer, I could see that the boy had pink-fuzz cheeks that told me he had never shaved. The woman was heavy, her dark hair tied back with a tight band. The boy's hands were empty. So were the woman's, but she had a leather sheath on her hip that contained a knife just short of being called a sword.

When they arrived at the gate to face me, I could see that the blond man's face had a leathery outdoor look and that his eyes were unsure about what they were looking at. One eye—his left—looked directly at me. The other eye looked off to the right. He reminded me of a lizard I'd seen in the Griffith Park Zoo.

"We help you?" asked the lizard, his voice low.

"I'm interested in the Survivors for the Future," I said. "I'm looking for Lawrence Timerjack."

"You just found him," he said. "You interested in joining us?"

"Might be."

"Mind showing me your wallet?"

I took out my wallet and handed it to him.

He flipped it open, looked at it with one eye, then back at me. The woman and boy and the other man hadn't stopped staring at me expressionlessly.

"Private investigator," he said.

"We like to survive, too."

"We're not a joke, Mr. Peters," said Timerjack.

"Okay," I said. "One of your members was arrested yesterday for murdering his wife with a crossbow. He said he learned how to shoot it from you."

"Pigeon Minck," Timerjack said.

He pronounced it "Pidg-ion."

"He called me a little while ago," Timerjack went on. "From the jail. Said you might be coming to see me. You carrying a weapon?"

"No," I said.

"You should. Come in."

He nodded. The boy and the woman lifted the log and pulled it toward them so I could enter. Then they put it back.

"Come," said Timerjack.

I followed him to the center cabin with the boy, the woman, and the other man behind me. With gravel crunching under our feet, we passed a green Ford sedan with dark windows. No one spoke till we got inside and the door was closed.

The room we were in was large. A desk with a blackboard behind it stood facing us across the room. A dozen metal folding chairs in two rows added to the schoolroom look. Detracting from it, however, was the array of weapons hung on hooks around the walls. There was a painting of an archer in green with a little green pointed cap. He had his bow pulled back and he was aiming at a boy with an apple on his head.

"William Tell," said Timerjack, moving to the desk and putting his bow and quiver on it. He had followed my gaze. "One of our patron saints."

The painting looked as if it had been copied from a poorly drawn comic book.

"Legend has it that after Tell shot the apple from his son's head, he went into the woods and defended himself from all attempts to capture him," said Timerjack, moving behind the desk and sitting.

I sensed the boy and woman behind me.

"What about the painting next to it?"

That one was of a man in a tan leather jacket and pants. He had an old rifle on his shoulder aimed at war-painted Indians running toward him. Their tomahawks were raised.

"The Deerslayer," Timerjack explained. "The ultimate Survivor."

"Impressive," I said.

"No, you are not impressed," Timerjack said. "But I'm not trying to impress you. If you had been trying to assassinate me or attack our compound, you would have been dead before your gun came out."

Timerjack nodded his head, and I heard a shuffling at my sides. As I turned, the boy whipped a thin bamboo tube from his pocket and the woman was pulling her knife from its sheath. The man with the shoulder holster and gun just stood there with his arms folded and smiled.

There was a whoosh of air as the knife shot past me and a thin shaft of wood or metal flew out of the tube the boy was holding up to his mouth.

The knife thudded into the William Tell painting, and so did the missile from the blowgun.

"Now are you impressed?" asked Timerjack, looking at me with one eye and at nothing with the other one.

"She killed William Tell's kid," I said. "So did he."

Timerjack smiled. It was a loony smile.

"That's what they were supposed to do, Mr. Peters."

"Now you've got holes in your painting," I said, as the woman went to retrieve her knife. The boy stayed behind me.

"We have others." Timerjack sat back and fished in his desk drawer.

He came up with a pipe and motioned for me to sit in one of the folding chairs. I had the feeling I was going to get lesson number one. The woman had a little trouble digging the knife from the wall, but she managed and gave me a less-than-friendly look as she returned to her spot behind me. I moved to the front row and sat. Timerjack nodded his approval.

I raised my hand.

"Yes?" asked Timerjack.

"May I go to the washroom?"

"Right through that door." He pointed toward a door to his right, but looked somewhere behind me. I didn't move.

"Forget it," I said. "It just seemed like the right thing to say to the teacher."

"Are you like this all the time?" Timerjack asked.

"Only when someone feeds me a good setup for a punch line. I do have some questions, a few of them about Sheldon Minck."

Timerjack puffed and nodded his head knowingly.

"Pigeon Minck has been with us five—"

"Six," the woman behind me corrected.

"Yes," Timerjack agreed with a smile. "Thank you, Martha. Six weeks. I'd say he's making slow progress in his skills, but we have no intention of giving up on him. He is a difficult project. We like the challenge."

"Progress in what?" I asked.

"Survival in the wild, in dark alleys, making and using weapons, blowguns, knives, clubs, spears, bows and arrows, crossbows and bolts, slings. We don't believe in guns."

"They exist," I said, looking pointedly over my shoulder at the craggy-faced man with the gun and holster.

"If other people make them." Timerjack ignored my look. "They need bullets made by other people, parts made by other people. When the time comes, we will be able to slip into the woods here or anywhere and survive. Of course, in these times, we make exceptions."

Now it was his turn to look at the man with the gun. "You mean Pathfinder Anthony. Even Natty Bumppo was forced to use a gun," he added.

I ignored the inconsistency and raised my hand again.

"You don't have to keep raising your hand." Timerjack was irritated.

"How many of you are there?" I asked.

"That is restricted information. We don't want our enemies to know our numbers."

From the size of the compound and the number of folding chairs, I guessed we were talking about twelve or fifteen.

"Your enemies?"

"And yours, too." He pointed the stem of his pipe at me. "The government, foreign powers. Indians. We live on a ridge along the Slough of Despond in the Valley of Despair."

"Indians?"

"They've been secretly conspiring for nearly a century to take back the land," Timerjack said. "Like Magua and the Hurons, they'll coordinate their move at night taking out the president, the cabinet, Congress, the governors, and generals. They're already in place."

"I didn't know there were that many Indians left," I said.

Timerjack smiled knowingly.

"We'll thwart them," he said. "When we have enough people, we'll thwart them; but just in case, we must learn to survive."

"The next Indian attack?"

"The next effort to destroy our resistance, to enslave us. It could come from almost anywhere."

I could have said, "You're nuts," and added, "Good-bye and keep your arrows sharp," but I had a mission.

"Maybe you've got a point," I said.

"You don't believe that," he countered. "I've gotten where I am because I can read people."

Where he was, as far as I could see, was three log cabins, some homemade weapons, a gun or two and about a dozen people wanting to buy into a religion of survival.

31

"What about Jews?" I asked. "Negroes?"

He shook his head. "You don't understand. The Jews are too smart to want to take over. There aren't enough of them, and they're doing fine the way they are. Hitler's an idiot, a con man. While he's been busy killing harmless Jews, the British, Russians, and Americans have been killing Nazis. Negroes don't have the capacity to constitute a threat. They don't have the will, with a few exceptions. Negroes are nothing to be afraid of. Waste of effort. They just let out two more of those Scottsboro Boys after thirteen years. Two more of them are still in jail. They didn't do it. Pigeon Minck is a Jew. Pathfinder Jackson is a Negro. We have no prejudices here. We are all human beings determined to survive."

"Pathfinder?" I asked.

"Our levels," said Timerjack. "Pathfinder Lewis will explain."

This time the pipe stem pointed over my right shoulder and I turned as the baby-faced boy said, "Pigeon. Bumppo. Pathfinder. Deerslayer."

Timerjack gave a smile of approval. It was pretty much what Shelly had told me. The boy smiled back and looked at me. It was the look and smile of someone Mrs. Plaut would call "simple of mind."

"You beginning to understand?"

I was beginning to understand that he was a loony and belonged in a loony bin, but I had a dentist to try to save.

"How good is Shelly with a crossbow?" I asked.

"Pigeon Minck is improving by the week." Timerjack examined the bowl of his pipe.

"Improving?"

"When he started, he couldn't hit the broad side of a large barn. Now he can. I'm not talking figuratively here. I'm talking about an abandoned farm through the woods over there."

He pointed to his right, looked that way with his right eye and at me with his left.

"So, what would be his chances of hitting a person about twenty yards away from him?"

"Given amazing luck or lots of tries, it would be within the realm of possibility."

"You willing to say that to the police?"

"I don't talk to the police. They come for me, and I go to the woods. I'm ready."

"But not to save Pigeon Minck?" I asked.

"I'll take it up with . . . I'll think about it. Pigeon Minck took the oath. He knows that the survival of the individuals in our group takes precedence over the survival of a prisoner of war."

"Who taught him how to use the crossbow?" I asked.

"I did, and Deerslayer Helter," he said, pointing this time at the woman.

I turned to her. She didn't look at me.

"Deerslayer Helter used to be a Catholic nun," Timerjack said.

"Mind if I ask Pathfinder Helter a few questions?"

"No," said Timerjack, "but don't expect any answers. She's taken a vow of silence in penance for a violation."

I was going to ask what the violation had been, but decided it might take me down a path with a pathfinder that I did not want to follow.

"Other people here have crossbows?" I asked.

"We all do," Timerjack said. "We all learn to use whatever weapons we might be called upon to take up."

He stood up suddenly, emptied the tobacco from his pipe into an ashtray, pocketed the pipe, and announced, "Four o'clock. Judo in Fortress One. Care to join us, Mr. Peters?"

"I'll watch."

"No," he said. "Our lessons are open only to members. I want to know if you want to join us, become a Pigeon, and learn to be a survivor. Special rates this month. Three hundred dollars to register. Eighty-five a month after that."

"I can't afford to survive." I stood up.

"We can work out a payment plan," he said, coming around the desk and handing me a pamphlet with a rough green paper cover.

"No, thanks." I pocketed the pamphlet.

"Didn't think so," he said with a sigh, picking up his bow and arrow. "But remember where we are and pray that you have enough warning to get to us when you realize that the enemy is in the streets. You forgot something."

"What?"

"Twenty-five cents for the pamphlet."

I dug out a quarter and handed it to him. He grinned.

"There's hope for you yet," he said. "You've just taken the first small step. It starts with curiosity and ends with commitment."

Pathfinder Helter held the door open for me, and I went out of the house of the mad tea party into the sunlight. The quartet ushered me up to the gate and watched as I got into the Crosley.

"I'll call before I come next time," I said through the open window.

"We don't have a phone," Timerjack said.

"Of course," I said and drove away, not looking back at them.

CHAPTER

4

DANGEROUS THOUGH THE journey was through streets that might suddenly be filled with war-painted, hatchet-wielding Hurons, I decided to go to my office to read the pamphlet. I also wanted to do some checking on Timerjack and talk to our receptionist, Violet Gonsenelli.

The trip was also dangerous because I had to get up to my office on the sixth floor of the Farraday Building without being drawn into Manny's Tacos on the corner, get through the lobby to the elevator or stairs without running into my landlord, Jeremy Butler and, most important, avoid an encounter with Juanita the Seer from New York City.

Parking was easy. A spot was open on Hoover, a few doors down from the building entrance. It was too small a spot for anything but a Crosley.

Traffic wasn't bad for a weekday afternoon, partly because of the gas shortage.

It took me about ten seconds to fail to get past the first obstacle in my path to my office.

I was hungry. I smelled tacos. Through the window of Manny's, I saw a businessman in a neat suit with a briefcase on the counter eating a taco special. I went in. The businessman was the only customer. The businessman ate solemnly, taking small businesslike bites.

Manny stood behind the counter, his potbelly covered by a white apron. Manny was smoking a cigarette and reading the newspaper. His son was fighting Nazis somewhere in Europe, and Manny had become an expert on the war thanks to the *L.A. Times* and the radio updates by Drew Pearson, William Shirer, and H. V. Kaltenborn.

The radio was on, a swing version of "Is You Is or Is You Ain't My Baby?"

I sat a few stools down from the businessman, and Manny looked over his newspaper at me.

"Two and a Pepsi," I said.

"Right," Manny answered, folding the newspaper and putting it neatly down on the counter.

"Big battle in the Pacific," he said from the grill. "Seventeen Jap planes, two freighters, one cruiser blown to hell."

"We lose any?" I asked.

"Four planes. Boyington's missing."

Major Gregory "Pappy" Boyington was the 31-year-old ace credited with shooting down twenty-six Japanese planes. The young man from Okanogan, Washington, headed the Black Sheep Squadron. His twenty-six enemy planes tied him with Major Joe Foss and World War One's Captain Eddie Rickenbacker.

"Got a bad feeling about it," said Manny, placing a plate with two hot tacos in front of me.

"We should have used gas on Tarawa," Manny said. "The *New York Times* says so. The *Washington Times-Herald* says so, and I say so. Lot of American kids got killed there. International law says it's okay to use gas. The Hague back in 1899, Geneva in 1925. Saves lives."

"Maybe," I said.

"Maybe, hell," Manny said. "You know how many casualties we have in this war?"

He picked up the paper and started reading aloud. The businessman turned his head toward him.

"Dead Americans, 29,650. Wounded, 41,050. Missing, 32,072. Prisoners of war, 28,732. That comes to 131,504. And when we invade Japan, those numbers are gonna look like peanuts. I say we gas the Jap army."

"And they gas us back?"

"We've got more gas." Manny was confident.

I had already taken my second bite of taco when Manny brought my Pepsi in a bottle.

The businessman finished his taco and reached for his wallet. He put down a dollar and some change and said to Manny and me, "Do either of you know a dentist in the office building a few doors down? A Dr. Sheldon Minck?"

Manny looked at me and I looked back. The businessman went on, "I was just at his office. There was no one there. Couldn't find the building manager's office."

"I know him," Manny said, picking up his paper.

"Have any idea who I could talk to about getting in touch with Dr. Minck? It's important."

"I think I could find him," I said calmly, finishing off the first taco.

The man moved to the stool next to me and held out his right hand. I wiped my hand on a napkin and we shook.

"My name is Verte, Desmond Verte," he said. "I'm a lawyer."

"He *has* a lawyer," I said.

"No," said Verte. "I don't want to represent him. I have something to deliver to him, and I need a signature."

"He's indisposed," I said. "I could get it to him. I share office space with Dr. Minck."

"Sorry." The man put his hand flat on the briefcase in case I tried to pick it up and run out the door.

"Well, in case I talk to him, what do you want me to tell him?"

The man fished out a business card and handed it to me.

"My name and phone number," he said. "Have him call. Tell him the Greenbaum and Gorman Company in Des Moines is very interested in discussing and entering into negotiations with him about the patent he holds for an anti-snoring appliance."

Shelly had patented about forty of what he called "major advances in dental technology" over the past decade. Almost all of them were either too painful or too wacky to draw any interest, though Shelly was always certain the next invention would lead to fame and wealth.

"I'll have him get in touch with you," I said.

Verte shook my hand, picked up his briefcase, said, "Thanks" and added that he would only be in Los Angeles for another four or five days and could be reached at the Roosevelt Hotel.

When he left, Manny lowered the newspaper and said, "Charles H. Warner died yesterday over in San Marino. He was seventy-one."

"Charles H. Warner?"

"Co-inventor of the automobile speedometer," said Manny. "Made him rich. Maybe Minck has something this time."

"Maybe," I said, finishing my second taco and downing what was left of my Pepsi. "He may become the richest prisoner in the state."

"Ironic," said Manny flatly.

"Ironic," I agreed.

"That's life. What the hell," Manny said, turning the page on his newspaper while "I'm Getting Sentimental over You" came on with the radio announced by Tommy Dorsey's trombone. "Heard on the radio that they played that song at the Paramount Theater on Broadway in New York yesterday. Gene Krupa's first appearance since his parole from San Quentin on those drug charges. Got a standing ovation. Krupa cried. Now they're playing it all day. My niece says Krupa is the grooviest hipcat."

"Hepcat," I corrected.

"You figure it out." He shook his head. "Guy takes drugs and everybody loves him."

I thought of suggesting that we gas San Quentin, but I didn't think Manny would be amused. And since I ate there a couple of times a week, it probably wasn't a good idea to test the cook's sense of humor.

I left a buck on the counter, fingered Verte's card in my pocket, and went out into the afternoon, heading for the office.

I made it through the dark entryway and into the eight-story-high atrium lobby with its familiar iron railings around each floor, its rickety iron-barred elevator and its familiar smell of Lysol.

A serious-looking pretty young blonde with what appeared to be a script in her hand hurried past me. The usual symphony of creaks accompanied me when I started the elevator. As I rode upward, laughter and shouting echoed off each floor, and there were sounds of music from a few of the offices where lessons were given.

I made it to the office of Sheldon Minck, D.D.S., S.F.C., L.M.O., on the sixth floor. Most of the initials under Shelly's name on the pebbled glass of the office door had no meaning. My name was in much smaller letters: Toby Peters, Confidential Investigations. I changed the wording from time to time, but not as often as Shelly changed the initials.

I expected, based on Verte's story, to find the door locked. But it wasn't, and the lights were on. Violet was sitting behind her little desk in the tiny reception/waiting room.

She was pretty, in her early twenties. She was also waiting for her husband Rocky to get back from the war. He had been a promising middleweight. I wondered if he'd have any fight left in him when he got back.

Violet looked worried.

"A man was here," she said.

"I know."

"I had the door locked," she said. "I didn't let him in. Then I thought, hey, I can't just hide in here forever so I opened the door, but he was gone. How's Dr. Minck doing? You see him? He all right?"

"He's all right," I said. "I'll be in my office."

"La Motta's fighting Fritzie Zivic." She looked down at a sheet of paper on her desk, pencil in her right hand.

"I'm not betting," I said.

Violet had completely destroyed my confidence as a boxing expert. She was a dark-haired temptress who rivaled those mermaids who lured sailors to their death. I didn't want to listen to her.

"Suit yourself."

"Okay," I said. "What's on the table?"

"I take La Motta. You take Zivic. La Motta wins in five or less or you win the bet," she said.

"Zivic's going to get knocked out in five or less?"

"Five or less," she said, still not looking up. "Even money. Five dollars."

I had Joan Crawford's money. I couldn't resist. Zivic could easily go more than five rounds. He even had a good shot at winning. The odds were seven to five for La Motta.

"Five dollars," I agreed.

She looked up, smiled, and held out her right hand to shake. I took her hand. She had a firm grip.

I reached for the inner door.

"Jeremy's waiting for you in your office," she said.

"How long?"

"About ten minutes. He was here earlier, too."

I nodded and went into the big room that was Shelly's office. The lights were out. The place looked clean and ready to rent. A dental chair and stainless-steel table stood in the middle of the room. An X-ray machine with a flexible arm and a cone with a glass in the middle that made it look like a hostile Martian took up space, too. There were metal cabinets against the wall to the right, and a double sink to the left, by the door to my office.

The place lacked something. It lacked the presence and racing emotions of Shelly Minck. I went to my door and opened it. The light wasn't on, but there was plenty of light from the single window. The former storage closet was just big enough for my small desk and chair and two extra chairs. The walls were decorated with a large painting of a woman with an infant in either arm and a photograph of me and my brother when we were kids with our father between us, an arm around each of our shoulders. At my brother's feet was Kaiser Wilhelm, Phil's German shepherd.

In one of the chairs, more than filling it, sat Jeremy Butler. He was the owner of the Farraday, a former professional wrestler turned poet who lived with his wife, the former Alice Pallice and their two-year-old daughter, Natasha, in an apartment on the eighth floor.

At sixty-five, Jeremy was a mountain, a solid bald mountain with a calm but battle-bruised face.

"How you doing, Jeremy?" I asked, moving behind my desk.

"Well," he said. "You've seen Sheldon?"

"I've seen him." I settled into my chair, dropping the pamphlet Timerjack had given me on the desk and facing him. "He says he didn't kill her. I believe him. He doesn't lie well."

"Is there anything I can do to help?" he asked.

"Not right now unless you know something about these people." I held up the pamphlet.

Jeremy reached into his pocket and came out with his glasses. When they were settled on his nose, he reached for the pamphlet and I handed it to him.

"I've heard of them," he said.

41

"From Shelly?"

"And Professor Geiger. I think it was Professor Geiger who told Sheldon about Survivors for the Future."

Professor Alan Geiger had an office two doors down from ours. He sold and gave lessons on the Aeolian trafingle. From time to time when I was on the hall landing outside the office I could hear the weird sounds of the machine. The Aeolian trafingle was played not by blowing into it, banging on it, or passing one's hands over it like a theremin. The trafingle produced music when a hand gently brushed one of a dozen bright aluminum rods sticking up from a square metal box. I had never yet recognized any melody that issued from Geiger's office.

"I'll talk to him," I said. "Is he in?"

"Yes," said Jeremy, returning the pamphlet. He also handed me a sheet of paper, neatly typed.

"It may have something to do with Dr. Minck," he said. "I dreamt last night this building crumbled and fell and that somehow the fault was mine."

He got up and added, "Anything I can do, remember?"

"I'll remember, Jeremy," I said.

When he closed the door, I looked down at the poem he had handed me. It was titled "Disappearing Houses."

> In English cities and small towns, weather,
> factories and the tread of man have worked
> To wear away the homes of peasants and kings.
> Yet there and where unbombed in Europe
> Are still homes of high and low, lived in,
> their wood worn, stones smoothed
> by four or five hundred years of man and God.
> Brick, wood, stones, some rescued from Roman ruins
> with telephones and radios and temporary furniture
> leaving the essence of what once still stood.

Why so different here where a century of standing
is deemed a miracle and little plaques are placed
on solid California homes whose sole distinction
is that they have survived for a single century?
And we are loath to have our personal history
Endure for more than three generations?
We live where nothing's meant to survive,
Not our homes, cars, the tools with which we work,
Friendships, loyalties, dedication, principles.
Today's history is tomorrow's nostalgia.
Today's friend is a remnant of only yesterday.
And so I attend to friends, homes and work places
keeping them alive as tribute to what can
endure rather than that we will not have stand.

The next time I saw Jeremy I'd tell him I found the poem moving and deep. Actually, I liked the ones that rhymed better.

I got up, turned off the light, went out the door, through Shelly's office and into the reception room. Violet was on the telephone saying, "Dr. Minck had an emergency. . . . No, he's not out of town, but it might keep him locked in for a while. I can pencil you in for an appointment in a few weeks and let you know if he's back."

While she talked, I took a pencil from her desk and wrote on the back of an envelope that I was going down the hall to see Professor Geiger. Violet turned the envelope around, read my message, and nodded, saying to the person on the other end of the line, "Yes, if you really can't wait, I can recommend my dentist. . . . No, Dr. Minck is not my dentist."

I left the office and closed the door. Two doors down was the office of Alan Geiger, professor of the Aeolian trafingle. I heard something inside, a twanging and a falsetto voice singing "Honolulu Baby." I knocked.

"Come in."

I opened the door. The professor was seated on a chair by the window of his large studio-office. He had a ukulele in his hands. There were chairs around the room, and in the center stood the bright metal box with rods reaching for the ceiling.

"Therapy, respite," Geiger said, looking down at the ukulele with a smile.

It was hard to take Geiger seriously, not because he was dedicated to his musical creation, the trafingle, but because he looked so much like Larry Fine, the one of the Three Stooges with the bald head on top and the curly fringes that stuck out on each side. The professor's hair was more or less tame, but it was still hard to shake the image.

He was dressed in a suit and string tie.

"I know you." He pointed the uke at me. "You have that little office inside Sheldon Minck's. You're . . . don't tell me . . . Tony . . . No, it's right on the door. I pass it every day. Tony Peterson."

"Toby Peters," I said.

"Right."

He put down the uke and crossed his legs. He continued to smile.

"You're interested in learning the Aeolian trafingle?"

"No," I said. "I'm interested in Lawrence Timerjack and the Survivors for the Future."

Geiger was not smiling any more.

"Why?"

"Because you told Shelly about Timerjack and he joined them. Now he's in trouble. The police think he killed his wife with a crossbow in Lincoln Park."

The professor uncrossed his legs and stood up, moving in front of the metal box in the middle of the room. He flipped a switch and there was a quick piercing electric buzz, replaced immediately by a low hum.

"I warned him," Geiger said. "I told him I had been a member of the Survivors for a few months. They taught me how to eat roots and build and use a blowgun. I quit after I almost swallowed a dart. Horrible experience. While I was choking, I could hear Timerjack talking to that woman about how they would hide my body. I coughed out the dart and walked out the door."

"Why would that story make Shelly want to join them?"

"I don't know," Geiger said with a shake of the head and a tentative touch of one of the rods of the machine in front of him. There was a humming sound. He ran his hand along the rod and the humming sound rose and fell. Then he began to adjust the dials. "Has to be perfect or it won't be under control."

"Why would Shelly join them if . . . ?"

"Ask him," he said. "I think the idea of making and handling weapons, being part of such a group intrigued him. He was looking for something to belong to. I was the unfortunate bearer of the tale that drew him in. Had he talked to a defrocked priest, he might have converted to Catholicism. You want to try this?"

He gently touched an upright rod with his left hand. The machine hummed in a wave of sound.

"No, thanks," I said.

"My biggest problem is that people keep comparing my creation to the theremin. They are nothing alike. The Aeolian requires putting one's hands on the tonal bars and, unlike the theremin, a skilled performer can imitate any instrument that exists and many which do not. It is a hands-on instrument, not a hands-off instrument.

"My rates are reasonable," Geiger said. "And for low payments over an agreed-upon period of time you could own your own Aeolian trafingle with individual lessons provided. It's the musical instrument of the future."

"I'll think about it," I said. "What do you know about Timerjack?"

"Know about him? He's cuckoo. He's nuts. He's dangerous. If you ever meet him . . . "

"I have," I said.

"That eye? Got hit in the head with a baseball when he was a kid. They wouldn't let him in the army in the first war."

"Because of the eye?"

"Because he was nuts. And maybe because of the eye a little, too. Who knows? He tells everyone he recruits that he's a master of the ancient and reliable weapons, but I never saw him actually use one. He carries them around, tells other people what to do. I made it to Pathfinder the day before I almost choked on that goddamn dart."

"That camp he runs by the lake," I said. "What does he charge members?"

"Not enough to keep the place going." Geiger touched a small rod on the Aeolian trafingle. "Want to hear me play 'Trees'? Sounds just like a mandolin."

"Another time," I said. "Where does he get his money?"

"Father owned Waldecker's Fishing Lures," said Geiger. "You know, 'the lures even the smartest trout can't resist.' Dad's dead, but they're still selling lures, and half the money goes to Timerjack."

"The other half?"

"His sister, Martha Helter. Even between them, I don't think we're talking about more than four or five thousand dollars a year."

"Helter? The ex-nun?"

"Ha," said Geiger. "And 'ha' again. She was a nun in another crackpot religion. The family is loaded with crackpots. I've got a copy of their pamphlet here somewhere if you want to read it."

"No, thanks. I've got one."

"If it makes any sense to you," he said, "please don't come back here and try to explain it."

"Anything else you can tell me?"

"Lots, but not about Timerjack and his pack of lunatics and misfits."

"Did you learn to fire a crossbow?"

"Yes," he said with pride. "And I was pretty good with it. It's not that hard."

I thanked him, moved toward the door and heard the start of a version of something that might have been "Avalon" creep up my spine.

When I got back to the office, Violet said, "You had a phone call, a woman. She said to call her back right away. Her name is Billie Cassin. She left this number. And your brother called. And Mrs. Plaut called and told me to tell you not to forget to stop for the groceries. And Martin Leib called. It's been a busy fifteen minutes."

I took the sheet of paper Violet had written all the names and numbers on and headed for my office.

CHAPTER

JOAN CRAWFORD WANTED me to know that she would have to go the next morning to an eight in the morning lineup to identify Shelly.

"Someone's bound to recognize me," she said.

"I'll make a call and see if I can keep it confidential," I told her. "After the lineup we'll go to Lincoln Park. I'll pick you up at seven-thirty."

She agreed, but she didn't sound happy about the whole thing.

Marty Leib was on another line when I called his office. I opened my window and waited for him and listened to the traffic going up and down Main and Hoover. I considered opening a few bills, but decided to doodle instead. I doodle a terrible Bugs Bunny. His teeth are too big and his ears droop.

"Peters." Leib's slow deep voice now came on. He spoke slowly because he billed by the hour, and Shelly was definitely going to pay for an hour for this call. "We have a good case, primarily because I think we can demonstrate that Sheldon Minck is incapable of seeing much of anything fifteen feet ahead of him, let alone delivering an arrow to the heart."

"Bolt," I said.

"Yes, right. I've got to remember that. Let me write that down. You need to find out two things. First, what was Mildred Minck doing in Lincoln Park at that spot at that time? Sheldon claims he didn't expect her there, was sure she had no way of knowing where he was."

He paused.

"Second thing?" I prompted.

"Second thing is to find out who might want Mildred dead. Besides Sheldon Minck."

"That it?" I asked.

"That's it. Oh, if you can find out who did kill Mildred Minck and how they managed it, prior to my entering a plea on Monday—providing it wasn't Sheldon Minck—it would be very helpful."

He hung up.

My last call was to my brother Phil. I had his direct number at the Wilshire Station. He answered after one ring.

"Pevsner," he said.

"Peters," I answered.

"Doctor called," he said. "Doesn't look like Ruth will make it through the weekend."

"I'm sorry, Phil."

"Yeah. I'm taking off for the hospital now. Ruth's sister Becky is taking care of the boys and Lucy."

"What do you want me to do, Phil?"

"The right thing," he said. "Yeah, and I've been suspended without pay for a week. The commissioner reviewed my file, had the chief in full uniform in his office, and strongly suggested that I seriously consider retirement."

"What are going to do?" I asked.

"Give it serious consideration." He hung up.

It was close to five o'clock. I'd had a busy day, but it wasn't over. I told Violet she should go home and went out the door.

Juanita was just getting out of the elevator, blue dress with a white sash billowing, long dangling earrings jingling, makeup doing little to cover her seventy years, but a lot for the cosmetics industry.

There was no way to escape.

"Toby," she said. "You've got one hell of an aura today. I'm telling you."

"It's been one of those days." I moved toward the stairs.

"It's been flowing out of your office," she said. "More like puking, if you know."

Juanita had left Brooklyn five years earlier, but Brooklyn had never left her. She dressed like a gypsy and had the accent of a Chock Full o' Nuts waitress. Most of her clients were Mexicans, young and old. There were a few Anglos in there, too, but not many. A sprinkling of Greek, Italian and Creoles rounded out her clientele, people who believed in her powers but probably didn't understand her any more than I did.

Juanita had found her gift long before she became Juanita, when she was still a middle-aged Jewish housewife who had just lost her third husband.

"I tried to ignore it," she once told me with a shrug, "but when you've got the gift, what can you do?"

"You're going to warn me again, aren't you?" I asked, trapped.

"I'm gonna tell you what I saw or sort of saw, you know what I mean?"

I didn't, but I just stood there waiting.

"You're looking for someone who carries a . . . I don't know, something dangerous. You're looking for someone who hurt some-one. No, killed someone. I see lots of dark green and purple. Death. You talked to that person you're looking for today."

"I don't suppose you could give me a name."

She put her hands on her hips. The fingers were covered with large rings. She shook her head.

"You know it doesn't work like that, for chrissake."

"Sorry," I said.

"Be careful," she said. "Someone is going to spit at you."

"How can I be careful about someone spitting at me?"

"I don't know. I figure if someone is going to try to spit on me I want to know it," she said.

"Anything else?"

"I see you in a big room, like a ballroom, something. You've got a gun in your hand, a funny-looking gun with a long barrel. Someone gets shot, killed."

"Me?"

She shrugged and said, "Who knows? I tell you what I see, not what it means. I'm a seer, not a philosopher."

"Is that it?"

Juanita stood silently for a couple of beats, sighed deeply and said, "Someone's aura is dimming. Someone you're worrying about. Someone who's dying I think. A woman."

"And what do I do about it?"

"*Veis ich?*" she said with another shrug. "How do I know?"

"Is that it?" I asked.

"I think so." She moved in front of me and put her hand on my shoulder. "No, there's a big change coming in your life, very soon, a new direction, a move."

"I don't want a new direction," I said.

"You don't want. Like you've got a choice here. You know Joan Blondell filed for divorce from Dick Powell today. She read a little poem she wrote to the reporters."

Juanita fished into her pocket and came out with a newspaper clipping. "Listen to this. Here's what Blondell wrote:

"Life is phony with baloney
From the start till it's done;
Gold or tatters, neither matters,
For the strife of Life is fun!"

"Thanks, Juanita," I said, starting down the metal stairs. "Jeremy might appreciate hearing it."

"Hey," she said. "Joan Blondell's right."

I could sense her on the sixth-floor landing, leaning over, watching me, listening to my footsteps rattle downward.

"The spit is sharp and purple," she called and her voice echoed through the six floors to the skylight. "It's coming soon."

I headed for the grocery with Mrs. Plaut's list. Back in October, a woman named Fannie Rager in Gettysburg, Pennsylvania, tried to fill out a ration-application blank. She tried, failed, and hanged herself. I knew how she felt, but I protected myself by turning over all my rationing paperwork to Mrs. Plaut. She loved filling out the forms and adding comments to the Ration Board in the margins. Sometimes she wrote in family recipes or advice on nutrition.

I had the ration stamps in my pocket and the list in my hand as I went down the aisles with a bag. I was reaching for a can of peaches when the can spat at me. A hole suddenly appeared in the can and syrup shot out of the hole. I jumped right and just missed getting syruped.

I looked around to see if someone had witnessed this miracle, but I was the only one in the aisle. I found myself looking at a sign for Campbell's Vegetable Soup. A cartoon balloon was next to the picture of a round rosy-cheeked Campbell Kid wearing ice skates. The balloon announced, "I'm pretty spry as you can see 'cause there's good soup inside of me!"

There was also peach syrup on the Campbell Kid's face.

When the spray stopped, I reached for the punctured can and looked at the hole. It looked like a purple tuft of cotton was plugging the hole, trying to keep back the flow of syrup. The can was sticky. The hole was narrow, but something just barely pro-truded from it. I grasped the tuft of whatever it was with two fingers and tugged at it. It came out easily, attached to a sharp pointed sliver of wood about five inches long.

"What happened here?" a voice said behind me.

I turned to face a skinny teenager with freckles wearing an apron. He was looking at the puddle of syrup on the floor and at the can in my hand.

"I think someone just tried to kill me with a blowgun," I said, holding up the needle-shaped piece of wood.

"Like so much Wheatena!" the boy said angrily. "You were sucking out the juice, and you were gonna put the can back on the shelf turned around."

"Does that happen?" I asked.

"Even crazier things, and I have to clean it up. You're paying for those peaches, mister. I hope you've got the cash and the stamps."

I dropped the little dart in my shopping basket and started toward the front of the store, being careful not to slip in the pool of syrup.

"I plan to tell Mr. Jerinetta about this," the kid said behind me.

At the front of the store, I looked around hoping to see some-one suspicious, particularly a Pathfinder with a blowgun. I moved along looking down each aisle. There were about a dozen cus-tomers, none of whom seemed to fit the bill.

"Did a kid just run out of here?" I asked the cashier, a string-bean of a woman with a red ribbon in her dyed blond hair.

"Someone ran out," she said. "Might have been a kid. I wasn't really looking. Gladys, you see someone run out of here a few minutes ago?"

Gladys, dark, chubby and a kid herself, was the cashier on the other aisle.

"No," Gladys said.

I put my groceries on the counter in front of the woman and looked out the store window. I saw nothing out of the ordinary.

"This stuff is sticky," she said, touching the container of Old Dutch Cleanser.

"Peach syrup," I explained. "Someone tried to kill me with a dart, probably poisoned. Hit the peach can, instead."

I held up the dart.

She looked up at it and me and shook her head. She was used to angry customers. She merely rang me up, took my coupons, put my groceries in a brown sack.

I headed for the door. Behind me I heard her say, loud enough to be sure I heard, "Hey, Glad, watch my checkout for a second. I gotta wash my hands and the counter. Some nut just syruped the place."

I went carefully to my car, opened the door and put the groceries inside. I placed the dart on the seat next to me on top of an old *Popular Science* magazine with the drawing of a monorail Train of the Future on the cover.

Someone had either tried to scare the hell out of me, or kill me, or maybe just inflict a little warning pain. The question was "Why?"

Best guess was that someone didn't want me trying to help Shelly. Looked at one way, this was a good thing. It meant that someone else had probably killed Mildred.

I pulled out into traffic with my windows closed and turned on the radio. A girl was singing something that sounded like opera.

I had another thought. Why had whoever it was shot at me with a dart? Why not hit me on the head or blow a hole in me or cut my throat or . . . I didn't want to follow this particular line of thought.

The girl on the radio now stopped singing. The drowsy voice of Major Bowes came on after the applause, saying that *The Original Amateur Hour* was always pleased to discover such talent and reminding us that we had just heard "'The Bell Song' sung by little Miss Louise Hornerhoven of French Lick, Indiana."

Major Bowes also informed me that Miss Lily Pons, who had made "The Bell Song" famous, had an entry in the Madison Square Garden Poultry Show.

"A silver-faced Cochin hen named Gilda Rosina," the Major droned. "And I was informed just before we went on the air that another great opera star, tenor Lauritz Melchior, has won a prize at the show with his cock named Great Tristan."

The studio audience applauded wildly, Miss Louise Horner-hoven of French Lick now forgotten.

I headed for the boardinghouse. At Mrs. Plaut's was someone I had to talk to about crossbows and darts.

CHAPTER

GUNTHER WHERTHMAN TOLD me to come in when I knocked at his door. Gunther was probably my closest friend. He was certainly my nearest neighbor, one door down from me at Mrs. Plaut's.

Gunther had lived in the boardinghouse before I got there, and when I helped him—he had been wrongly charged with murdering a Munchkin on the set of *The Wizard of Oz*—he convinced me to move into a room chez Plaut.

Gunther worked out of his room, a tasteful den with a desk, full bookshelves lining the walls, two comfortable armchairs and a small bed in one corner near the window.

The bed was small because Gunther doesn't need a big one. He is three feet tall.

When I entered, Gunther was at his desk, pencil in hand, pad of paper in front of him next to his typewriter. Gunther made a good living translating books and articles from or into any of several languages. He worked for government agencies, big businesses and publishers. He wore three-piece suits and Windsor-knotted ties even when he had no plans for leaving Mrs. Plaut's.

"News of Dr. Minck?" he asked with only a trace of his native accent.

"Doesn't look good," I said, sitting in the armchair facing him.

I had dropped off the groceries downstairs with Mrs. Plaut. She had told me that I had done a satisfactory job but that I was late.

"Someone tried to kill me with a blowgun in the grocery store," I had said, holding up the dart.

She had peered at it over her glasses. "Don't go to that store anymore," she said.

I told her I wouldn't, and she handed me some sheets of lined paper filled with her distinctive handwriting, clear, clean, small, and invincible.

"This is a singular adventure," she said, nodding at the pages. "It marks a crucial moment on my father's side of the equation, a moment which might well have resulted in my father not being born."

"I see," I said.

"How can you, Mr. Peelers?" she asked. "You haven't read it yet."

I had long ago given up any attempt to convince Mrs. Plaut that I was neither an exterminator nor a book editor. I had some theories about how she had come to this conclusion, all of them connected to being almost deaf, unswervingly determined, and able to reconcile almost any contradiction that came her way.

She had been better since Gunther and I had given her a hearing aid, a Zenith Radionic, forty dollars, complete with radionic tubes, crystal microphones, and batteries. She had been better when she chose to wear it, which was seldom. Mrs. Plaut was somewhere over eighty years old and sometimes mentally over the rainbow. A broom handle of a little woman, she was strong, tireless and impossible to resist.

"Snuggle in and read it tonight," she said. "After dinner. Dinner is at six twenty-seven. Please inform Mr. Gunther."

I looked at Jamaica Red in his cage. He was busy pecking at his little glass bowl of seeds.

I had gone upstairs, bypassed my own room, and gone straight to Gunther's, where I now sat.

"Dinner's at six twenty-seven," I said.

Gunther nodded in acceptance, and I held up the dart.

"Know what this is?"

Gunther put on his glasses, got down from his chair, and approached. I handed him the dart, saying, "Be careful. There may be poison on the tip."

He took it carefully.

"Blowgun," he said. "I have seen darts like this before. Pietro Guilermo, the knife thrower in the Romero Circus, had a blowgun. He was a very versatile performer. The circus was small. When he threw knives, he wore a gypsy costume and earrings. When he used the blowgun to pop balloons, he covered himself with black makeup and became Zumbugo of New Guinea."

"He ever use a crossbow?"

"No." Gunther turned over the dart.

"Ever have a live target?"

"Yes. Me. Remember, the Romero Circus was small. I was primarily an acrobatic clown, but I helped with the other acts."

"What can you tell me about blowguns and crossbows?"

"Very little, I'm sorry to say. But I know someone who can tell you anything you want to know, August Blake at the Southwest Museum. He is an expert on ancient weapons. If you like, I'll call him."

I told Gunther that I'd like to talk to August Blake as soon as possible. Gunther reached into the inner pocket of his jacket, came up with a leather address book and found the number he was looking for.

"I will be back in a moment."

There was a small stool near the phone on the landing. Gunther stood on that when he used the wall-mounted pay phone. I stayed in the chair. Gunther was back in about five minutes.

"August Blake is on the phone. He can see us at eight at the museum. Would that be acceptable?"

"Eight is perfect," I said.

This time Gunther was back in less than a minute.

"The museum is open till five," Gunther said. "But August is working late tonight on a recently unearthed Mayan discovery, a double-edged ax never before considered a Mayan weapon or tool."

I thanked Gunther, went to my room and clicked on the floor lamp. The room hadn't changed. Next to the closet on my left was my bed, neatly made up with the little pillow Mrs. Plaut had given me, which bore the words "God Bless Our Happy Home." Because of my unreliable back—the gift of a large Negro gentleman who had once given me a bear hug—I always pulled the mattress to the floor when I slept. I had to sleep on my back on something reasonably firm.

The large man who had done the damage to my back had wanted to talk to Mickey Rooney at an Andy Hardy premiere. I had been hired for the night to protect the star.

Each morning Mrs. Plaut woke me, looked at my position on the floor, closed her eyes, and shook her head at what she considered my eccentricity.

"I assume," she had said the first time she discovered me that way, "that this is part and parcel of your religious practice. I respect the rites of all castes and sects, but you will have to return the mattress to the bed each morning you engage in this practice."

And that is what I did.

Next to the window was a small wooden table with two chairs. Behind it was a refrigerator and another table on which sat a hot plate and an Arvin radio. Near the lamp was an armchair with lace doilies carefully placed on each arm of the chair, a dresser with a Beech-Nut Gum clock on the wall over it. The clock told the right time. My father's watch on my wrist was seldom within a two-hour range. The Beech-Nut clock said I had about fifteen minutes to get downstairs for dinner.

The window was open. Dash, an orange cat to whom I sometimes belonged, sat on the ledge looking at me. There was a tree next to the window with a branch that almost touched my sill. Like me, he came and went whenever he pleased. I was always good for some milk and occasional cans of tuna or pieces of chicken filched from Mrs. Plaut's table.

I went to the refrigerator and got some milk while Dash waited patiently. I had time to grab my dopp kit, go to the bathroom on the landing, wash my face, shave with my Gillette, brush my teeth with Teel, get my kit back in my room, and make it down the stairs and into Mrs. Plaut's rooms, where I assumed my place at the communal table.

"Punctual," Mrs. Plaut said from her chair at the table near the kitchen.

Gunther sat at my right. Across from us were the other boarders: the one-armed car salesman Ben Bidwell and Mrs. Plaut's shy and pretty niece Emma Simcox. Miss Simcox was in her thirties, a light-skinned, pretty Negro. Mr. Bidwell was a ruddy-faced lean man in his forties. Bidwell and Simcox had begun to keep company. They were a good match. She hardly ever spoke, and he hardly ever stopped speaking.

"Hmm, smells great," Bidwell said, looking at the food on the table.

On a platter in front of us was a platter of baked macaroni with five flat rectangular browned slices of something familiar-looking on top.

"Spam," said Bidwell, smiling at Emma Simcox.

"Prem," Mrs. Plaut corrected. "Like Swift's Premium Ham, it's sugar cured. Made with Parmesan cheese, margarine, highly nutritious, lots of protein, and B-complex vitamins."

It didn't smell bad, and I was hungry. Mrs. Plaut nodded for her niece to serve herself, and the meal began. Dinner conversation consisted primarily of Ben Bidwell assuring us that right after the war the price of new cars would be about nine hundred dollars "unless you want to go for one of the luxury models General Motors is planning. They'll hit as much as fourteen hundred."

The vegetable for the meal was boiled beets, and dessert was steamed farina molasses pudding which, Mrs. Plaut proudly announced, cost a total of thirty-four cents.

Gunther and I excused ourselves after dessert, and Mrs. Plaut reminded me to be sure to read the new pages of family history she had given me.

In the car, we listened to Joan Davis on *Sealtest Village Store*. Joan, in her cracking voice, was telling Mr. Heinzwig the butcher to "trim the fat, get rid of the water, and keep your thumb off the scale."

The Southwest Museum was on Marion Way and Museum Drive overlooking the Arroyo Seco and Sycamore Grove.

My father had taken my brother and me to the opening of the museum in 1914. It was memorable because it was one of the few Sundays he had taken off from working in our small grocery store in Glendale.

Thirty years later, the museum looked just the way I remembered it, a white concrete building without ornament, a tile-roofed tower at one end and a high, square tower at the other.

We parked in the lot and walked through the entrance, a brightly colored Mayan portal designed, as Gunther now informed me, in the manner of the entry at the House of Nuns at Chichen Itza in the Yucatan. Inside the portal was a long tunnel, 260 feet long, according to Gunther. It led into the base of the hill on which the building stood. Dioramas on each side of the illuminated tunnel depicted the history of the primitive Asian migrants who millennia earlier had settled the western American coast.

At the end of the tunnel stood a man. Behind him was an elevator, its doors open.

"Good evening," the man said, his voice echoing eerily down the tunnel.

August Blake was around sixty, with white hair. A solid block of a man with a clean-shaven face, he gave us a Santa Claus smile of greeting.

He held out his hand. Gunther and I shook it in turns, and Gunther introduced me.

"Come," said Blake, stepping back so we could enter the elevator.

The doors closed behind us after we entered, and we faced front. Blake said, "The lower lobby is one hundred and eight feet above us."

It took about twenty seconds before the elevator stopped and the doors opened.

"The lights are dimmed," he explained as we stepped out. "Museum's closed, the blackout, money saved."

The lobby was a broad room lined with American Indian exhibits. There was something ghostly about the shadows, the musty smell and the faint sounds of creaking.

Blake led the way to a stairway in the center of the room. We walked up to and through a room marked "Plains Indians." We passed a tepee.

"Blackfeet, Cheyenne, Crow and Arapahoe," said Blake with pride, his voice and footsteps still echoing. "Clothing and weapons. The weapons are my particular interest."

He guided us into the south wing of the building and past the closed doors of an auditorium. "Torrance Tower," he said, opening a door through which we followed him. "My office is this way, past the library."

About thirty feet farther, we stopped at a door with Blake's name on it in black letters. Inside the room it was bright, a contrast to the darkness we had just been led through.

There was a large cluttered desk in one corner and an even larger table in the center of the room. On it were bones, bows, arrows, something that looked like a peace pipe, and large, open books. There were also three magnifying glasses and a microscope. The walls were floor-to-ceiling bookshelves.

Blake led us to the table.

"You have it with you? The dart?"

I removed it from the handkerchief I had wrapped around it. He took it and turned it. Held it up to the light. He picked up a magnifying glass and examined it slowly.

"Blowguns have been around for more than 40,000 years," he said, looking at the dart. "Popped up all over the world. Serendipity. The hand of God or gods. This dart is made from river cane, *Gigantis arundaris*, probably the same material the blowgun that shot it is made of."

"Poisoned?" Gunther asked.

"No. No need. A blowgun three or more feet long with a ten-inch dart in the hands of a Cherokee hunter could be shot accurately enough to pierce the eye of a deer at fifty feet. African tribes and South Sea Islanders used poisons in battle and hunting. But this isn't a hunting dart."

"What is it?" I asked.

"Too short, suggests a short blowgun, probably two feet. Could still be deadly accurate from twenty feet or even more. Person who made this dart knew what he—"

"—or she," I said.

"Never heard of a woman using a blowgun," Blake said with a smile. "But why not? Good lungs, steady hands, a hard blow. Person who made this ground the point the way it's supposed to be. Amateurs whittle. This purple fluff on the end—"

He held it out for us to look at.

"It's called fletching. This one is cotton, light, fluffy, fills the hole so there's something to blow against."

"What do you know about crossbows?" I asked.

He handed me the dart, and I rewrapped it and returned it to my pocket.

"Ancient and primitive weapons of all manner are my passion," he said. "Along with chocolate ice cream. What would you like to know?"

"First," I said, "how accurate are they?"

"Remarkably in skilled hands," he said. "By 1330 in Europe they were making prods—"

"Prods?"

"Springs," he explained. "Of steel with pulls of fifty pounds and much more. Deadly at distances well over one hundred and fifty feet."

"Are they hard to make?"

"Not if you know what you are doing," he said. "It's relatively easy to buy plans for crossbows, or to buy them already made."

"The things they shoot—bolts, quarrels, whatever," I said. "Are they all pretty much the same?'

"No," he said. "Different lengths, designs, even special specifications for the avid user."

"Is there any way of telling if one of these bolts came from a particular, I mean, a specific crossbow?"

"You mean like ballistics with a bullet? No, but if you show me a bolt and a crossbow, I can tell you if that bolt was shot from that specific design of crossbow."

I looked at Gunther. He didn't seem to have any questions.

"Thanks," I said. "Would you be willing to testify in court as a crossbow expert?"

Blake beamed.

"Murder case?" he asked.

"Yes," I said.

"Sure."

I thanked him. He ushered us back to the tunnel, shook our hands and got back in the elevator.

Dinah Shore sang "April in Paris" to us in the car as we headed back to Hollywood and Mrs. Plaut's.

Back at Mrs. Plaut's, I got undressed, put on a pair of clean boxer shorts, pulled the mattress to the floor, and sat in my armchair reading Mrs. Plaut's pages:

THE EPISODE OF THE SILVER CREEK GHOST

He is said to have had a small but distinctly purple wart on the end of his nose, which was the only distraction from what was generally agreed to be a face rivaling that of the infamous but handsome male members of the Booth family, particularly Edwin not the one who shot Mr. President Abraham Lincoln. My grandfather Wallace Edward Hamilton Simcox whose name was longer than he was tall since he is reported to have been no more than five feet and three inches in height even before he shrunk from the natural mystery of age.

My grandfather resided in Silver Creek, Colorado with my grandmother and their two sons, Wayne and Warren. My grandfather was the foreman of the December Silver Mine, a very responsible job.

It is reported though I don't remember it myself that my grandfather was weak of eye, fond of the bottle and possessed no sense of direction often walking two miles the wrong way to work though he traversed the self same road for more than twenty-five years.

One night after stopping after work at the Horseback Saloon to get quite stinking drunk which he felt was his right and obligation as a hard working man once a week, he recalled that he had left a lantern burning near a shaft. He had done no such of a thing but the recollection had come to him in his cups.

Mason Thurling, who made a meager but honest living cleaning the spittoons at the Horseback, had volunteered to accompany my father back to the mine to be sure he went in the right direction. All in the Horseback thought this an idea of merit. We are talking about a barroom filled with drunken louts who would not know an idea of merit were it branded on their bicuspids and they could taste it.

Mason Thurling was the town drunk in a town of drunks, an accomplishment of no small stature.

And so they proceeded back to the December on a moonless night. They discovered no lamp left lit and in the darkness Mason tumbled over a wheelbarrow and went unconscious. My grandfather stumbled toward the mineshaft and was about to step into it when the ghost appeared glowing in front of him.

Stop you goddamned fool the ghost so said to my grandfather who stopped.

The ghost so my grandfather said afterwards looked exactly like Dolly Madison though when questioned my grandfather could not give accurate information on where he might have seen Dolly Madison's image.

My grandfather took several steps back and tripped over Mason Thurling who awoke with a start seeing the ghost. Mason's hand was broken in the incident and was of little use from that night forth forcing him to become left handed and change his profession to that of itinerant harmonica player along with a hare-lipped Indian who played a broad repertoire of Stephen Foster tunes.

Due to his repute as a drunk there were few who believed Mason's confirmation of the sighting of Dolly Madison's ghost. However it must be recalled that my grandfather would have certainly been smashed to blood and bone had not he seen the ghost or vision. Dead he would have been unable to return home where that very night my grandmother conceived my father William which led to the birth of my mother Dolly Madison Simcox which led to me Irene named not for a ghost but a seamstress who had not taken the gesture of my being given her name as payment for a dress.

I turned off the lights, got on the floor with a pillow under my head and closed my eyes. And the dreams came. Two I couldn't remember, but the last one—that one I remembered.

I was in Cincinnati. I don't know what I was doing in Cincinnati. I don't know why I dream about Cincinnati. I've never been to Cincinnati, but the Cincinnati of my dreams is a vast city without people.

It was night. Street lights were on. I was standing in front of the door of a modest one-story brick house. The door opened slowly. I wanted to back away but my legs wouldn't move. Over my shoulder a voice whispered, "Oh-oh, now you're in for it, bub." I turned my head toward the voice. It was Koko the Clown. He nodded his head toward the door letting me know I should pay attention.

The door was open all the way now. The house was dark inside, but a woman stood glowing in front of me. She was wearing a Colonial costume complete with bonnet. In her hands was a crossbow. She was aiming it at me. I knew she had to be Dolley Madison.

I tried to think of something to say to her, something to stop her, to assure her I voted for her husband, that I'd once been to Madison, Wisconsin, and walked down Madison Avenue in New York.

She raised the crossbow higher. It was pointed at the top of my head. I reached up and felt an apple balanced in my hair. Koko snatched the apple and took a big bite, and Dolley Madison lowered the crossbow. It was aiming at my chest now. I knew her finger was tightening on the trigger.

"I told you you were in for it, bub," Koko said, and a bright light hit my face and a woman's voice said, "Time."

I opened my eyes. Mrs. Plaut stood in the doorway of my room, the hall light behind her.

"Time," she repeated. "It's seven."

I left Mrs. Plaut's a few minutes later and hurried to pick up Joan Crawford.

CHAPTER

THE ROOM, THE size of a small storefront shoe store, was dark except for the low platform at one end bright with overhead lamps. Folding chairs sat facing the platform. I was sitting on one side of Joan Crawford. Marty Leib was sitting on the other. Tony Sheridan, an assistant district attorney, sat directly behind us. There were also two plainclothes detectives and a couple of uniformed cops.

"Okay?" asked one of the plainclothes detectives.

Sheridan, tall, lean, and recently discharged from the army after two Purple Hearts and a case of battle fatigue, said, "Okay."

I had picked Crawford up at her house just after the sun came up. She was wearing a plain black dress and a floppy hat with a big brim and dark glasses. She did her best to hide her lack of enthusiasm about my Crosley and got in the front seat.

"Phillip is home with the children," she said.

It was Saturday.

I started driving.

"He wanted to come, too, but if both of us were there, we'd have to get someone to watch the children, and the likelihood of my being recognized would certainly be increased."

"I understand," I said.

"Do you?" she asked, looking at me while I drove. "What do you think of when my name is mentioned?"

"Movie star," I said.

"Yes, movie star," she said, finding her cigarettes and lighting one. She didn't ask if I minded. I did, but I didn't say so. There wasn't much room in the Crosley, and cigarette smoke makes my eyes burn and gives me a headache.

She sighed.

"Mr. Peters"—she half-turned toward me—"I come from a very poor family. My formal education ended with the fourth grade. I've been singing, dancing and acting my heart out since I was ten years old. I don't know how to do anything else. I don't want to do anything else. Yes, I'm a star, and I intend to remain one. Are you certain there will be no reporters today?"

"You see the *Times* this morning?" I asked, eyes on the road.

"No," she said.

I handed her the folded copy shoved alongside the seat on my left.

"Page three, bottom left," I said.

She took the paper, turned the page quickly, and folded the paper in half. She read it to herself. I knew what it said under the headline, which read: **Dentist Kills Wife in Park with Crossbow.** The article said that Sheldon Minck, a dentist, had shot his wife to death with a crossbow in Lincoln Park. The article also said Shelly and his wife were "estranged" and that he claimed he was in the park practicing. The only other piece of information of interest was that there was a witness who was passing by when the killing took place. There was no mention of Billie Cassin or Joan Crawford.

"This is good," she said with a slightly relieved smile.

"Good, but not perfect," I said. "Even if there are no reporters at the lineup, one of the cops may recognize you and tell a reporter."

"You can stop that from happening?"

"I called Shelly Minck's lawyer this morning. He'll be there. He said he'd try to make some kind of deal with the district attorney's office."

"A deal?"

"If Shelly pleads guilty, your testimony won't be needed."

"He intends to plead guilty, doesn't he?"

"I don't think so," I said. "The other possibility for a deal would require my finding who killed Mildred fast, before you have to be in a courtroom where there would probably be a reporter or, if not, there would definitely be people who'd sell the information to the closest reporter for a few bucks."

"I see," she said. "So . . . "

"I've got to try to find the murderer fast."

We didn't say much more. I wanted to turn the radio on and listen to anything, but I didn't.

"Very well," she said. "If you become certain that this will appear in the press or on the radio, let me know and I'll do what I can to salvage . . . No, it can't come to that. I can't let it."

The last was said with such determination that I turned to look at her. I saw the face of a woman I wouldn't want to tangle with. I couldn't see her eyes behind the sunglasses. I didn't think I wanted to. She was wearing makeup, but not much, and it was possible that with only a quick glance, she might not be recognized.

"When we get there," I said, "take off the glasses, don't walk fast, and don't smile. I'll go in first. You follow."

"And the point of this?" she asked.

"To keep from drawing attention to you and to give me a chance to spot anyone who might be a problem."

We were almost at the Hall of Justice now, and I didn't want to answer more questions than I had to.

"Problem? You mean like reporters, a fan?"

What I meant was "like a pink-faced kid with a blowgun," but I only said, "Right."

She went silent, thinking, smoking, and giving me a headache.

"What if I don't identify this Dr. Minck?" she asked.

"They won't believe you," I said. "The D.A. will give you lots of trouble, and they might even decide to have a not-very-nice but very long talk with you."

"I see," she said. "Well, let's go."

We went. So far everything had gone reasonably well. Now we sat in the dark while five men were paraded onto the platform and told to face forward with their backs against the dirty white wall.

Shelly was facing us at the end of the line to our right. He was wearing a blue shirt and an expression of openmouthed blinking bewilderment. He took off his glasses and squinted into the darkness in front of him.

"Number five," said one of the detectives. "Put your glasses back on."

Shelly put the glasses back on.

Next to him was Jerry Pants, a pickpocket I recognized, who was two inches shorter, thirty pounds lighter and about a decade younger than Shelly. Jerry Pants looked bored. He had played this game many times before. In the middle of the lineup was a cop whose name I didn't remember. The cop was tall, in good shape, and blank of face. Next to him was someone about Shelly's shape and age, who even had a bald head and wore glasses. The glasses weren't as thick as Shelly's and I'd give five-to-one they were plain glass. He was a dark-skinned Negro. The last man in line, at the far left, was lean with a wrinkled face, large eyes, and a grin that revealed a very small number of teeth. He bounced from one foot to another, either practicing a dance step or needing the bathroom.

"Now take your time," Sheridan said behind us. "Look at them carefully."

"Tony," Marty said with a sigh. "This is supposed to be a line-up, not a sideshow."

"You wanted the lineup, Martin," Sheridan said evenly.

"Miss Cassin has already given a description of the man she saw in the park," Marty said. "There should be *five* men up there who fit the description, not one."

"We get who we can get," Sheridan said. "Well, miss?"

"The one on the far right," John Crawford said, her voice a little higher than normal and her accent that of a Southern belle, or at least one in a movie.

"Number five, step forward," the cop called out.

No one moved. Pants put his hand on Shelly's shoulder and Shelly said, "Who me?"

"You," said the cop.

Shelly shuffled forward.

"You sure?" Sheridan asked over her shoulder.

"That's the man," she said. "I gather he hasn't confessed to his crime."

"He hasn't confessed," said Marty slowly, "because he is innocent."

"You can go now, miss," Sheridan said. "We'll be in touch if we need you further."

Crawford rose, her face averted from cops and Sheridan, and followed me out of the room.

"They recognized me, didn't they?" she asked as soon as we were in the empty hallway.

"Marty and Sheridan? Yes. Marty won't want you to testify in a trial court. Who would doubt the word of Joan Crawford?"

She laughed.

"You might be surprised," she said. "I've lied with great sincerity to a great many people, primarily men, and even on occasion to myself."

"You'd make a great prosecution witness," I said, walking with her to the elevator. "My guess is Sheridan'll figure he's better off keeping this one as quiet as he can. He's not ambitious. He doesn't like reporters."

"But if Dr. Minck's lawyer and Mr. Sheridan do not come to an agreement . . . "

"You're out of the bag, which is why we're going to Lincoln Park now."

Marty Leib called out, "Wait," before the elevator arrived. We turned to watch him move slowly toward us.

"Nice suit," I said.

Marty nodded and looked at Joan Crawford.

"Miss Cassin," he said with a smile that said he clearly knew who she was. They shook hands. He didn't let hers go. "I represent Dr. Minck, the man you just identified. I'd like to talk to you for a few minutes."

"Well . . . I—"

"Dr. Minck has asked to see Mr. Peters. While he's doing that, you and I can spend a few minutes together, please."

He still held her hand tightly.

"I don't bite," he said with a smile.

"I do," Crawford answered, pulling her hand from his angrily. "Do I have to talk to him?" she asked me.

She was my client. Shelly was my friend. Marty was Shelly's best chance at getting out of this with minor burns. I was his second-best chance.

"I think it would be a good idea," I said.

"Very well," she said. "Where?"

Marty stepped back and held out his right hand, palm up to show her the direction.

"I'll meet you at the car in ten minutes," I said.

"More like twenty," Marty said.

"Fifteen," I said.

"I suggest we stop haggling over my time," Crawford said, definitely irritated. "I'll get there when I can, and I intend that to be very soon."

She walked a few steps ahead of Marty so he could get a good look at her legs. Grable might be the pinup girl with the gams, but Crawford's matched hers and more. Besides, Grable was pregnant now, and there hadn't been a new pinup of her in two years.

The elevator came. I went to the visitor's room, checked in with the guard, and sat in the same chair as the day before. This time there were two other prisoners with visitors. One pair included the fat Negro man from the lineup. On my side of the mesh his visitor was an equally fat Negro woman with a straw purse perched in front of her on the counter. The other duo comprised an older guy whose white hair needed combing and who was listening to a man in a suit with slicked-back hair.

They brought Shelly in, and he sat across from me.

"You know what just happened to me?" he asked.

"I was there," I said.

He did a triple squint and opened his mouth.

"I'm a dead man, Toby," he said. "Tell me, tell me the truth, I'm a dead man."

"You ever hear of Greenbaum and Gorman in Des Moines, Iowa?" I asked.

"They're involved? Now they're making electric chairs and gas chambers?"

"I don't think so, Shel," I said. "What do you know about them?"

"Toby, can we please concentrate on trying to save my life here?"

"I've got good news," I said.

Shelly stopped fidgeting and looked at me in anticipation of a reprieve.

"What?"

"Greenbaum and Gorman want to talk to you about your anti-snore gizmo."

"My . . . Greenbaum and Gorman? They're the biggest. . . . Most of my office equipment comes from them. I'm going to be rich," he shouted with a laugh. "I'm going to be rich." Then his voice dropped. "And I'm going to be dead or in prison. You know what irony is?"

The white-haired prisoner, whose head was still down said, "The agreement between two parties that an action or utterance which appears to be one thing is perceived by both of the parties and perhaps others as carrying a meaning other than that which appears on the surface."

Shelly and I both turned to look at him. He was now looking up at us.

"Well," Shelly began.

" . . . taught English literature at U.S.C.," the white-haired fellow said. "Now . . . this."

"Thanks," I said.

Shelly, his voice now low, said, "Toby, you've got to help me here. I'm going nuts. I've only been here two days and the food is starting to taste good to me. I'm in a cell with two men who keep swearing at each other and threatening each other. And they keep having arguments, and they keep asking me which one of them is right. I try to even it out, but they both hate me. One of them is crazy. He eats shoe polish. *Brown* shoe polish."

"I'm doing what I can, Shel," I said.

"Well, do what you *can't,*" he said, looking around the room as if it had begun to close in on him. "What good is being rich if you have to spend your life in a cell with a lunatic who eats brown shoe polish?"

I had no answer.

"At least the food is good," I said.

"Actually, it's not bad," he said. "I'm worried about losing my patients, Toby."

"Try to keep calm, Shel," I said.

"Not 'patience,' 'patients,'" he said with exasperation. "I have people who rely on me for healthy teeth and gums."

And they now have a reprieve, I thought. Instead, I said, "I'll get you out of this. Just do what Marty says."

"Leib? He says we're going to claim it was an accident, and if that doesn't work, he'll plea-bargain and if that doesn't work, insanity. I don't think he wants to go to trial."

"Shel, when we tell him that Greenbaum and Gorman are interested in your snore gadget, he'll come up with other options."

Shelly shrugged.

"I gotta go, Shel," I said. "The woman who witnessed you killing Mildred is downstairs waiting for me."

"What? The one who identified me? Whose side are you on?"

"Yours, Shel. I'm going to try to convince her that you didn't do it."

"Didn't I?"

"Absolutely not," I said, trying to sound like William Powell doing Nick Charles. "I'll see you tomorrow."

Before he could say anything else, the white-haired man who used to teach English at U.S.C. said, "Technically, he didn't kill her with a crossbow. He killed her with a quarrel, or bolt fired from a crossbow. To kill her with the crossbow, he would probably have to beat her over the head with it."

The well-dressed man with the slicked-back hair adjusted his tie again and rolled his eyes toward the ceiling. I wondered what the professor was accused of—probably murder by boredom.

Joan Crawford was sitting in the Crosley. I had left the door open. Her window was down. Her floppy hat covered her eyes, and she was smoking.

"How well do you know that lawyer?" she asked when I got behind the steering wheel.

"I've used him," I said cautiously.

"I think he suggested that I lie about seeing Dr. Minck shoot his wife," she said.

"Wouldn't surprise me in the least," I said, moving into traffic.

"I will not be manipulated," she said firmly. "I will not perjure myself. I intend to tell the truth."

She was glaring at me again. I smiled.

"I wouldn't want it any other way," I said. "I didn't have breakfast this morning. You want to stop for coffee?"

She didn't say no, so I headed for the drugstore where Anita works behind the lunch counter. I was hungry. Mrs. Plaut had told me I had to stay for breakfast. I told her I couldn't. She was serving Eggs Benedict Arnold.

"A hearty breakfast is the key to a fruitful day," she had reminded me.

I had apologized, dressed quickly and got out before she decided to barricade the door and spoon feed me.

I had another reason for wanting to stop at the drugstore. Joan Crawford was Anita's favorite actress. *Rain* was Anita's favorite movie, but *The Women* was a close second.

Crawford flicked on the radio. We listened to *The Man Behind the Gun*. I had a headache.

CHAPTER

ANITA WAS AT the far end of the counter carefully slicing a pie in preparation for the lunch crowd. There were no customers at the counter, and she finished slicing the pie before she glanced up, saw me, smiled, and then noticed the woman at my side with a floppy hat and sunglasses.

Anita froze.

Now Anita is, as Mrs. Plaut once pronounced her, a head-on-her-shoulders, feet-on-the-ground woman, but the sight of Joan Crawford swept away her practicality.

I had known Anita for more than thirty years. I had taken her to our high-school prom in Glendale. I had lost track of her till a year ago, when I walked into this drugstore and ordered bacon, eggs, toast, and coffee on the twenty-five–cent breakfast special.

Anita had been married, widowed and raised a daughter. I had been married to Ann, divorced, no kids other than me. Aside from Carmen, she of the ample bosom and placid exterior, who spent her days as the cashier at a deli I no longer frequented, there had been no other woman in my life until Anita. I had fruitlessly and uselessly pursued Ann, who was now on her third husband, a movie actor whose name was known but whose movies didn't draw in big dollars. I wondered if Joan Crawford knew Ann's husband. I decided not to ask.

Anita wore little makeup, had dark blond hair, and carried her age on a good-looking open face that let you know the woman was ready for whoever walked through the door, be it an old boyfriend from high school or a movie star. But she hadn't been ready for Joan Crawford.

Anita wiped her hands on a towel, strode toward us behind the counter as we sat stood waiting.

"This is my friend Anita," I said.

"Pleased to meet you." Crawford held out her hand.

Anita took it briefly and shook. "I'll bet people are always telling you that you're their favorite movie star and they've seen all your movies," Anita said.

"That does happen rather frequently," said Crawford.

"Lucille Le Sueur," Anita said. "*Old Clothes* with Jackie Coogan. You and Jackie Coogan. The scene where he was crying and you hugged him. And *The Only Thing* with Conrad Nagel. Then you changed your name to Joan Crawford. That was in . . . 1925. Then you did the Harry Langdon movie and—let me think—*The Taxi Dancer* and the western with Tim McCoy. And one of my favorites, the one with Lon Chaney where he pretended not to have arms and then he cut them off so you'd love him and—"

"*The Unknown,*" Crawford supplied. "I believe you. You may be the first and only person who has seen all my movies."

"I haven't even gotten to the talkies," Anita said.

"I almost didn't either," Crawford said with a laugh.

"You want me to shut up?" Anita asked.

"No, dear," Crawford said. "I want you to bring us coffee and an ashtray."

When Anita was at the far end of the counter getting the coffee, Crawford whispered, "She's not a would-be actress, is she?"

"No," I said.

"I was a waitress when I was a kid," she said, removing her sunglasses. "It's not easy work. She's your . . . ?"

"Friend," I said.

Anita was back with the coffee and a smile.

"Pie? Peach. Fresh."

I said yes. Crawford said no. Anita got my pie.

"How many hours do you put in?" Crawford asked, drinking her coffee black. I doused mine with two spoons of sugar and milk.

"Six to eight, depending," Anita said.

"Feet and ankles," Crawford said.

"Feet and ankles," Anita agreed. "Can I say something?"

"Say," said Crawford.

"Why weren't you even considered for Scarlett O'Hara?"

Crawford stiffened for an instant, and then she said, "Mr. Selznick thought I couldn't sufficiently show Scarlett's underlying vulnerability."

"He was wrong," said Anita.

"You, my agent, and I agree, but I considered it a victory of sorts when Bette Davis was turned down for the role after telling everyone it was hers."

I knew Anita also liked Bette Davis, but I knew Anita was smart enough not to say the wrong thing such as mentioning that Davis later won an Academy Award for playing another Southern belle, the lead in *Jezebel*.

"What's your next movie?" Anita asked. "You don't mind?"

"I play a housewife who loses her husband, has to raise her daughter by becoming a waitress, and winds up owning a string of restaurants."

"You're not kidding?"

"No," said Crawford.

Some new customers arrived but didn't come to the counter. The coffee seemed to be helping my headache. I looked at my father's watch. Don't ask me why. Habit. Memory sought. According to the watch, it was ten after one. I knew it was off by at least three hours.

We finished, and I dropped a dollar on the counter.

"I read about Shelly," Anita said, glancing at Crawford.

"It's all right, Anita," I said. "Miss Crawford knows all about it. She's helping me try to clear him."

Anita looked confused. It wasn't a good time to enlighten her. I told her I'd call her later.

Crawford reached her hand over the counter and Anita took it.

"It's been a pleasure meeting you," Crawford said.

Anita simply smiled.

When we were back in the car, Crawford said, "Did you just use me to impress your lady friend?"

"Yes," I admitted.

"Good," said Crawford. "I like her. And now?"

"Lincoln Park," I said, stepping on the gas.

I parked in the lot off Alhambra as close as we could get to the path Crawford said she had taken. We walked past the eucalyptus-shaded picnic grounds, made a turn at the end of the six-acre lake, passed the merry-go-round, children's playground, the four horse-shoe courts and the conservatory of rare tropical plants.

We walked past benches and bushes along the path and made a turn. To our right about a hundred yards away, I could see the tennis courts.

"There," she said, stopping and pointing into the grassy field. There were a few trees, heavy with leaves growing randomly in the field.

"Show me where you were standing," I said.

"Right here," she said.

"And Shelly?"

"Approximately twenty-seven feet in that direction perpendicular to that tree and my hand," she said.

"Twenty-seven feet?" I asked.

"I've been studying camera distances for more than twenty years," she said. "I spent my free hours watching movies being made, watching feet being counted off, lights being adjusted, marks being set. Twenty-seven feet, give or take a few inches."

"Let's go."

She led the way to the spot, and I asked her where the target had been and where Mildred had been standing.

"She was moving when he shot her," Crawford said.

"Toward him?"

"Yes."

I looked around. To the left of the path behind us was a growth of bushes. Someone could have been in those bushes. Someone could have waited for a witness and then, when Shelly fired, he or she could have fired, too—not at the target but at Mildred.

"How big would you say this field is?" I asked, looking around.

"About sixty yards square, more or less," she said. "Why?"

"Let's look for a bolt," I said.

"Mr. Peters, I fail—"

"If someone else shot Mildred when Shelly fired, then somewhere in this field is the bolt Shelly shot."

"What if he fired more than one?"

"He said he only fired the one."

"Where do we look?" she asked.

"The logical place would be beyond the target or near where Mildred died. But given the fact that we are talking about the man for whom the word 'myopia' falls far short of reality, it could be anywhere."

"Or it could be nowhere. There might not be another bolt."

"Might not," I said.

We started to look. About fifteen minutes into the search, a skinny redheaded kid on a bicycle came up the path.

"Stop," I called out to him.

He started to go faster.

I flipped open my wallet with my private detective's license, which he couldn't see even if he were looking at us. "Police," I shouted.

He came to a slow, reluctant stop on the path and called, "You lose something?"

"Yeah," I said.

"Is it worth anything? Like a watch, a ring, money, you know?"

"Help us look, and, if you find it, I'll give you a buck."

The kid laid his bike on the edge of the path and came running toward us. He was about sixteen or seventeen, with his pants legs rolled up. His short-sleeved shirt had horizontal blue-and-white stripes. He nodded at Crawford, who nodded back. The kid was definitely not a fan of Joan Crawford movies.

"What are we lookin' for?" the kid asked.

"A piece of metal about this long, shaped sort of like an arrow. If you find it, don't touch it. Just leave it there."

"I've only got a few minutes," he said, starting to search. "I've got to get back to school."

"You come this way every day?" I asked.

"Pretty much," he said. "I've got an early lunch period. I bike home."

"You were here two days ago when the woman died?"

"I guess." He avoided my eyes.

"You tried to help."

"I guess."

"The fat little man with the thick glasses told you he thought the woman had a heart attack, right?"

"Yeah, but there was blood and everything. He started crying."

The kid shrugged and added, "She was dead. There wasn't anything for me to do here, and I didn't want to miss school."

"I'll write you a note. I need your name and address." I took out my pad. "And your phone number."

He said his name was Scott Kaye, and he told me his address and phone number.

We continued searching.

Ten minutes later, my back in pain, my head hurting, the kid found it. He pointed down at the trophy and grinned.

"You owe me a buck," he said.

I pulled a dollar bill from my wallet and gave it to him. He ran for his bike. The bolt was twenty yards left and about thirty yards beyond where Shelly had set up his target. Crawford joined me, and we both looked down at it.

I took out my almost-clean handkerchief, picked up the bolt, and put it in my jacket pocket.

"You're going to take it to the police?" she asked.

"Yes."

"They won't believe you. They'll say you're lying to save your friend."

"You're here with me," I said.

"I've been in enough mysteries to know that they'll simply claim you planted that bolt there and got me to come out with you till we found it."

"You have a devious mind, lady."

"I need it to survive in my business," she said.

"Well, they can check it for Shelly's prints. It convinces me that Shelly didn't do it."

"You could be wrong," she said.

"It's happened."

"Now what?" she asked.

"Now I find the real murderer of Mildred Minck."

"Now *we* find the real murderer of Mildred Minck," Crawford said. "And we do it before I have to make an appearance in court on Tuesday."

As it turned out, the arraignment of Shelly Minck was rescheduled for Thursday so that he could attend Mildred's funeral.

But that wasn't the only funeral I would attend in the next few days.

CHAPTER

MY SISTER-IN-LAW RUTH died the night Joan Crawford and I and the kid found the bolt from the crossbow in Lincoln Park.

I found out about Ruth after I had dropped Crawford off at her home and made it to Mrs. Plaut's just in time for dinner.

Gunther was waiting for me on the porch. He and Mrs. Plaut had been sitting on the porch swing. When I came up the concrete path, they both stood. I could tell someone had died. I wasn't sure who, but I had a good idea.

"Ruth?" I asked.

Gunther nodded.

Mrs. Plaut handed me a platter covered with waxed paper and said, "An egg and artichoke casserole. It serves five."

I took the platter. It was still warm.

"You are to go to your brother's house," said Gunther. "And, if you wish, I would like to accompany you."

"Come on," I said.

Mrs. Plaut waved good-bye to us.

We didn't talk as we went over the hills toward North Holly-wood. Gunther sat with the casserole in his lap. I turned on the radio. We heard the end of the Cab Calloway Show and all of *Abie's Irish Rose* before we pulled up to the house.

Casserole in hand, Gunther at my side, I walked up to the door and knocked. Ruth's sister Becky, a healthy, older version of my dead sister-in-law, opened the door. Her eyes were red, but she smiled when she saw me and said "thank you" when I handed her Mrs. Plaut's casserole.

The afternoon went slowly. Visitors were in and out, bringing food and condolences. Phil shook hands, accepting sympathy; the boys, Nate and Dave, were solemn, mimicking their father. Lucy, my four-year-old niece, was playing at a neighbor's.

There wasn't much to say, and not much was said for the four hours I spent mostly watching my silent brother, whose hands clenched and unclenched from time to time, wanting to strike out at someone or something.

It was a long four hours.

The funeral was the next day, Sunday. Phil wanted it done quickly, tastefully, and small. And that's what it was, because many of the people who might have wanted to come simply didn't have time to make it.

At the small storefront funeral home on Pico, Phil sat in the front row with Lucy on his lap. She had a stuffed Mighty Mouse in her arms and was gently touching its stitched-on eyes and paying no attention to what was going on around her. My nephews—Nate, who was almost fourteen, and Dave, who was ten—sat between Phil and me. The boys wore suits and ties and looked solemn and blank faced. Becky sat in the row in front of us. Ruth had no other siblings, and both of Becky and Ruth's parents were dead.

Most of the people in the small room sitting in front of the covered coffin were cops, a few were Ruth's relatives, and there were some mutual friends, including Jeremy and his wife Alice, Gunther, Mrs. Plaut, Anita, and Violet.

The doctors had been treating Ruth for three years, and she had just kept fading away, a different diagnosis pronounced by each specialist. Phil had refused an autopsy. He didn't care what had killed his wife. He cared only that she was dead.

Phil owned a funeral plot in a cemetery in Glendale. It was a few hundred yards from where our father and mother were buried. Phil's former partner, Steve Seidman, had handled the funeral arrangements, pulled strings, called in favors to get everything done quickly.

There was a shiny boxlike podium of dark wood on the platform behind the coffin. Since my brother and his family attended no synagogue or church, he wanted no last-minute pieced-together generic eulogy by a clergyman of any cloth. Jeremy said he would be happy to read a poem. Phil asked Becky to say a few words and did the same with Nate, telling him only if he wanted to.

Phil started the funeral service by saying only, "Thanks for coming. My wife, the mother of my children, the sister of Becky, the friend of all of you here, is gone. I don't know where she went. Not in that box. She spent a long time dying and too short a time living. She left a note."

He pulled a sheet of paper from his pocket and took a very deep breath. His hand automatically went up to his tie to loosen it as he did every working day. But he stopped himself, unfolded the sheet, and read:

"Phil, David, Nate and Lucy. Love each other as I have loved you. Live and make me proud of you. Grieve, but not too long. Remember me, but not with sadness."

Phil folded the sheet and returned it to his pocket. He looked down at the podium and placed both palms flat on it.

"That's it," he said. His voice didn't break, but it came close.

Becky and Nate spoke briefly, both saying they would miss her, that she was a good wife, sister and mother, and that she would be remembered.

Jeremy said he would like to read his poem at the cemetery and since Phil had no plans to speak at the burial, he agreed.

The sun was shining in the small cemetery in Glendale. We huddled around the casket which was perched on two low wooden sawhorses next to the open hole.

Jeremy, massive in a suit and tie, which I had never before seen him wear, moved to the podium and said, "This is 'A Melody for Ruth.'"

And then he read:

> There is no end but death.
> We look for start, middle and end
> To give our lives a diameter,
> Controllable limits that send
> Us a feeling of security
> Suggesting an order
> That may not be there.
> If there is a border,
> We create it; and sense
> Is just a matter
> Of which story we sing
> And whose song
> You remember the melody of.
> And we know the truth.
> We will remember the Song of Ruth.

When the casket was covered, I told Phil that I'd come over to the house later. Lucy clung to his neck, asleep.

Forest Lawn Cemetery was also in Glendale, just a few miles from the small cemetery where Ruth was now buried, a few miles in distance but in another dimension.

Forest Lawn is 303 acres of smooth green lawn with no tombstones—just bronze tablets. It does have mausoleums for the famous and wealthy who want and can afford them. Forest Lawn is surrounded by the world's largest wrought-iron fence and gate. The $4,500,000 mausoleum-columbarium, inspired by the Camposanto in Genoa, rises in terraces not far from Babyland, where only infants are buried. Buried or sealed in Forest Lawn are, among thousands of others: Jean Harlow in a chamber purchased by William Powell, Tom Mix and John Gilbert. Irving Grant Thalberg is inside a private mausoleum, and Lon Chaney is buried in an unmarked grave because too many fans visited and trampled the ground.

Begun in 1919 by Dr. Hubert Eaton, more than 87,000 people had been laid to rest inside its iron fence.

Dr. Eaton, known as "The Builder," still around and perpetually upbeat—partly because he was reported to be clearing two million dollars a year—was fond of saying, "I believe in a happy eternal life."

Forest Lawn's income came not just from interments but also from christenings, fifteen-dollar marriages, casket sales, and the peddling of life insurance.

Flowers and fountains were all over the place, and soothing recorded music came from speakers throughout the park.

The service for Mildred Minck was held in a massive chapel with a giant stained-glass window depicting *The Last Supper.* Sitting on a small table covered in blue velvet in front of the chapel was an orange fake-oriental urn.

Handcuffed to a detective, Shelly sat there, blinking at the nonsectarian service being read by a tall, lean woman minister in a white robe. The woman came with the service, like pickles come with a hamburger.

"Her smile lit up a room. Her laughter brought a smile to those in need of a smile," the minister said in a soothing, singsong voice.

I didn't remember Mildred ever smiling or laughing. To Mildred the world had seemed to be a very sour lemon on which she had been mistakenly placed to pucker and complain.

There were only eight other people in the large chapel and more than one hundred empty chairs. I sat at the back where I could see everyone.

"Faith, hope and charity were always in her heart," the minister went on.

I'll give Mildred "hope." She was always trying, but she had faith in nothing but the dollar, and charity to Mildred was definitely a foreign word used only by backward people.

To my left sat the Survivor quartet. Lawrence Timerjack, his right eye aimed in the general direction of the droning minister and his left fixed on me. He wore a black shirt with an orange tie and black pants over combat boots. Pathfinder Lewis, he of the pink cheeks and blowgun, sat on Timerjack's left. He, too, wore a black shirt and slacks but no tie. He slouched, arms folded, as he looked at the back of Shelly's head. To Timerjack's right, sat Deerslayers Helter and Anthony. Same black shirt and slacks, the dress uniform of the Survivors. With them were two more members of the group wearing black. One of the two was a young bull of a man with a military shaved head and a protruding lower lip. Next to him sat another man, about forty, with a head of full dark hair and a well-trimmed bushy mustache.

Professor Geiger, in no uniform but a droopy herringbone jacket, sat five rows in front of the Survivors.

Mildred had a brother. No one knew where he was. No one had known for as long as she had been married to Shelly.

There were none of Mildred's several lovers. No friends. Not even her hairdresser, who had taken an ample chunk of Shelly's money over the years. I take that back. There was a solitary man sitting alone near the exit door. He wore a sport jacket and tie and kept glancing at his watch. He looked a little like Warner Baxter.

" . . . to contemplate what good she may have done had her life not been ended at so young an age," the minister said.

Contemplating what hell she could have brought to Shelly and all who chanced to meet her would have been a more realistic enterprise.

I had called Marty Leib between funerals. He didn't have to bother to tell me that using his services on a Sunday morning meant double the per-hour fee. Shelly would be paying for it and, according to Leib, Shelly would soon be able to afford it.

"Good news, bad news, neutral news," Marty had said. "Which one first?"

Marty had talked to the company in Iowa that wanted to buy Shelly's snore-away device.

"It was a joy, Peters," Marty had said. "It started as negotiations and ended as an agreement to surrender. Sheldon Minck will get a cash payment of $172,000 plus one percent of the retail price of every device sold. The $172,000 will not be an advance against that one percent."

"Your cut?" I'd asked him.

"Ten percent," he said.

"Now the bad news?"

"No, let's do good-bad news," he said. "Mildred was worth a total, including jewelry, real estate, insurance from her parents' death a few years ago, of about $200,000. She left no will. Shelly gets the whole caboodle."

"That's good," I said.

"*And* bad. Motive, Peters, motive. Mildred had filed for divorce. If the divorce had gone through, whatever she had would now go to some distant relative, perhaps that long-lost brother. Have you got anything for me?"

I told him about the kid finding the bolt in the park. I told him what Shelly had said to the kid about thinking Mildred had a heart attack.

"And that's enough to convince you of Sheldon's innocence?" he asked.

"Enough," I said.

"Enough to convince me, providing we can prove the bolt you found was fired from Dr. Minck's crossbow and that he had not fired it earlier. Still, it provides some obfuscation. Not as much as a qualified ophthalmologist will, but something."

"It gets a little more complicated," I had told Marty. "I found out this morning that there were no fingerprints on the bolt we found in the park."

"I'll have to think about that one," he said.

We hung up. It was funeral time. First Ruth's and now Mildred's.

"The kingdom of the Lord in the Land Eternal," the minister was saying now, her arms outstretched, her robe hanging like wings. "And we all say—"

"Amen," the cop cuffed to Shelly said. The rest of us added our amens.

The woman in the white robe beckoned toward Shelly and the cop. They rose and made their way up the platform to the podium.

Shelly squinted out at us, cleaned his glasses on his shirt and said as he looked at the orange urn, "Mildred had good teeth and gums. You'll have to believe me, those of you who didn't know her, but I'm a dentist and I know good teeth. Heredity accounted for a lot of Mildred's dental health, that and hygiene."

The cop handcuffed to Shelly looked at his prisoner with an expression that suggested he thought he might just be needing backup.

"I didn't kill Mildred," Shelly went on. "At least, I don't think I did. Maybe I did. I know she's dead."

Someone in the audience—I think it was Martha, the Deerslayer—coughed. Shelly squinted toward the back row.

"My friends know I loved Mildred, loved her with . . . for her sense of humor, her beauty, her compassion, her . . . Well, not for her compassion."

Which, I thought, was as evidently nonexistent as her sense of humor and beauty. All that Mildred had lacked to make her picture perfect was snakes where her hair was.

"She left me. She took up with other men. That bothered me, particularly when she picked up with that little guy who she thought was Peter Lorre. You remember that, Toby?"

Everyone turned to look at me. I nodded to show that I remembered.

"See?" Shelly said. "And did I forgive her? For that? For everything? For taking the house, all the money in the bank accounts, the car?"

He was still looking in my direction. I nodded again. It wasn't enough for Shelly.

"Tell them, Toby."

"He forgave her."

"Mildred's favorite food was lobster tail," Shelly went on. "Her favorite writer was Pearl Buck. Her favorite radio show was *Big Sister,* though she liked Dinah Shore. Now she's in heaven. Mildred, not Dinah Shore. I'm sure Dinah Shore will go to heaven, but not for a long time."

Shelly looked at the cop who looked away, feet apart, eyes now forward, waiting.

"I met Mildred when I was in dental school," he said. "She came into the clinic. I cleaned her teeth and we fell in love. In spite of what some people said at the time, she didn't marry me just to get away from her father who was involved in bootlegging and was facing eight federal charges, as was her mother. We never had children. Mildred didn't like them. She said they don't clean under their fingernails, even the really good ones, unless they've got some kind of mental thing about keeping clean."

Shelly paused, his eyes moist. He took off his glasses and rubbed his eyes with the sleeve of his uncuffed hand. Then he faced us again and continued, "What was I saying?"

The cop whispered something to Shelly. Shelly nodded and, facing us again, said, "Amen."

We all repeated it. The cop started to lead him away, but the pudgy dentist stopped short and called out, "I'm not sure where I'll keep her ashes. I don't know if I can have them in prison, but if I don't go to prison, I'll keep Mildred in my office. I spend more time there than anywhere else. You can come and see her whenever you want. And since you've come to this service, I'll offer all of you a twenty-percent discount on all dental work."

This time the cop yanked Shelly from the platform and an unseen organ began to play "Coming Through the Rye."

The Survivors gathered at the rear of the chapel. Professor Geiger moved to the center aisle to put a hand on Shelly's shoulder as the cop hurried him out. Shelly gave me a pleading look. I smiled and winked and probably did something with my shoulder to suggest that I had everything under control.

When he was gone, I started toward the door. Lawrence Timerjack and the two burly mourners I didn't know blocked my way.

"Peters," he said, Lewis on one side, Helter on the other. "I intend to tell you something. I intend to tell it once. I intend it be acted upon or, maybe better, not acted upon. You understand?"

"No," I said.

"Peaches," said Timerjack.

I looked at young Pathfinder Lewis, he of the pink cheeks and the blowgun. Lewis grinned.

"Some people read tea leaves or palms," said Timerjack. "I read peach pits."

"And what do the peach pits say?" I asked.

"That you're all wet and sticky, and that if I wanted to make you more than just wet and sticky, well, you wouldn't have been here today to hear Pigeon Minck's heartfelt speech."

"So you want me to stop trying to find out who killed Mildred Minck?"

"I'm a straightforward man," Timerjack said. "Don't know how to be anything else. You'll find out anyway, so it's best if I'm straightforward with you."

"Find out what?"

"Dr. Minck's will left everything to his departed spouse. In the case of her death, which is the case, everything of Pigeon Minck's goes to the Survivors."

Which, I knew, meant a little under four hundred thousand dollars.

"But Shelly has to die for you to collect," I said.

"We do not want that," said Timerjack.

There was a long, long pause while Timerjack waited for me to figure something out.

"With Shelly dead, you get everything. With Shelly in jail, you figure you can talk him into giving you a lot of money."

"While we fight the government to free him from an unjust charge," Timerjack said. "If you meddle, anything could occur."

"Like Shelly going free and having time to think that being a Survivor might not be a very good idea?"

"We are prepared to hire you," Timerjack said. "Deferred payment when we start receiving money from Pigeon Minck. All you need do is two things. First, you stop looking for someone else who might have killed Mrs. Minck. Second, you help convince Pigeon Minck that I am his best hope for freedom."

"How much of a payment?"

"Five thousand dollars," he said.

"What if I said twenty thousand dollars?"

Timerjack glanced at Anthony at his side and then looked back at me.

"We would consider it," Timerjack said, now standing at parade rest. "Consider it seriously."

All of which suggested that Timerjack definitely knew about Shelly's no-snore deal and probably knew about Mildred's money.

"So will I," I said, stepping forward so that the two guards had to step out of the way or else put their hands on me. I look tough. I even work out at the downtown YMCA playing handball with Doc Hodgdon and punching the light and heavy bags.

The problem is that none of this assures me of winning a fight. My record would keep me far off the rankings of contenders in middleweight, my weight class. All of which means that I lost more than I won if victories were counted in blood, bruises, and broken body parts. But I had one thing going for me: I didn't give up. Whoever took me on or out, including the two bodyguards, were going to have to work like hell to keep me down and would be taking care of their own first-aid problems.

"Let me guess," I said. "These are the last of the Mohicans, Uncas and Chingachgook."

"Your knowledge of the canon is admirable even if your sense of humor isn't," Timerjack said, motioning for the two goons to let me pass.

Shelly and the cop were nowhere in sight when I left the chapel. I headed across the lawn to the sound of a rippling harp in the direction of the parking lot.

Had Timerjack just admitted to Mildred's murder? Not quite, but it was clear he wasn't going to make it a long mourning period.

My list of suspects was short. Considering Mildred's charm and taste in men, there had to be more.

The next stop was the house where Mildred had lived, sans Shelly, for almost a year.

CHAPTER

THE HOUSE WAS on Orange Grove just off Pico. It was a two-story red brick building with a sloped roof and two steps up to a cherry-wood door with a shiny brass knocker shaped like a lion's head.

Shelly had always wanted a knocker in the shape and color of a gold tooth, but Mildred had shot down that idea before he could even describe the tooth. His backup idea had been a curled mink, but Mildred had argued—reasonably, for a change—that not everyone would recognize it was a mink.

I didn't use the lion's head knocker. No one was supposed to be home. Mildred had changed the locks so I couldn't go to the flower bed on the side of the house for the spare I knew about. If there was a spare, I didn't have time to look for it, anyway.

My decision was simple. Shelly owned the house. Even if I were caught breaking in, I'd tell whoever caught me that I had Shelly's permission and, providing jail time had not turned his brain to apple butter, he would back me up.

I moved to the back of the house where the small yard was surrounded by bushes. I could see the neighbors' homes on both sides. There hadn't been any cars parked in the driveways or on the street in front of either of the houses.

I broke a small window in the kitchen as quietly as I could, reached in and undid the latch, pulled the window up, and climbed in. I was on the kitchen table slipping off a red-and-white checkered tablecloth. The cloth and I thumped to the floor.

Though I had known Shelly for more than five years, I had never been in the house before. Mildred didn't approve of me and, to be fair, she was right not to. But then again, I didn't approve of Mildred.

I got off the floor, put the cloth back on the table, and threw the larger pieces of window glass in the garbage can under the sink. They landed on some bunched-up and crumpled sheets of paper. I fished the paper out without cutting my fingers on the glass and unfolded them on the table.

There were three sheets.

The first one was addressed, "Dearest Mortimer." That was all it said. I put it aside. The second sheet was addressed to the *Los Angeles Times* and listed four suggestions to the editor including moving the war news off the front page because it was depressing, eliminating the stupid sports news, stop attacking President Roosevelt, and refunding her subscription money because the newspaper failed to cover three events about which she had informed them. There was a number five on the page, but Mildred had, apparently, decided to scrap the letter before she finished it.

The third sheet was a list of things to do. Each item had a line through it indicating, I assumed, that the task had been done. The list read:

Call Ferris and Paine about slowing down divorce.
Move hairdresser up to Monday to be ready for funeral.

Change dinner date with Jeffrey to eight o'clock Tuesday
   instead of Thursday.
Call the Randolphs and tell them you've decided not to sell
   the piano.
Change meeting with Leland to seven.

That was it. The item that interested me most was the hairdresser. Whose funeral was she planning for? I doubted it was for
her own. I also wondered why she wanted to slow down her
divorce from Shelly.

I put the first two sheets back in the garbage and pocketed the
list. That was when the music started.

"Somebody came and took her away," came the male voice
behind Tommy Dorsey's orchestra.

The music was coming from the front of the house. I had lots
of choices. I could dive through the window and probably put
myself in traction for a few weeks. I could open the door and run,
which might work, or I could do what I knew I was going to do.

I didn't have my gun. I seldom carried it. It was usually locked
in the glove compartment of my car. It wasn't that I was unfamil-
iar with guns. I'd been a cop, an armed security guard, and I was
a licensed private investigator. I was also a terrible shot and as
much a danger to innocent bystanders and myself as I was to
whomever I might be trying to shoot.

The hell with it. I went through the kitchen door, heading for
the music. It got louder as I stepped into the dining room. There I
saw a lightweight table of black-painted wood with thin metal legs
and six chairs that matched the table. Next to it was a black side-
board with silver handles on the drawers with a painting of
Mildred above it. At least I think it was supposed to be Mildred,
an idealized Mildred, a Mildred as played by Binnie Barnes.

I went through the dining room and into the living room. It
wasn't large and was almost all white with lots of chrome. In here

I found myself facing a man standing next to a Zenith phonograph. He was holding a small stack of records each in a brown paper sheath.

"Mildred loved these," he said, glancing over at me.

I recognized him. He had been the one who looked like Warner Baxter, sitting by himself at Mildred's funeral service. He was tall, wearing a definitely nonfunereal pair of dark slacks and a sporty lightweight dark green jacket with a white shirt and yellow tie.

"'Baby Face,'" he said holding up the record. "Sammy Kaye."

I took a few steps toward him. The closer I got, the older he looked. His black hair was definitely dyed, a good job, but Hollywood dyed. The tan looked real, but I wasn't so sure about the perfect teeth smiling at me as he held up a record.

"'The Wang Wang Blues.' Paul Whiteman."

"You want to dance?" I asked.

"With you? You're not my type." He grinned, shook his head, and held up another record. "'South America, Take It Away.' Xavier Cugat."

"How about Mildred? She your type?" I asked.

"Mr. . . . ?"

"Peters," I said.

"Mr. Peters, Mildred was most definitely my type. It wasn't just her charm, beauty, and brilliant wit that drew me to her. It was her generosity. I'll miss her."

"How did you get in?" I asked.

"I have a key."

He put down the stack of records. Tommy Dorsey did a solo on his trombone. We both listened.

When it was finished, he lifted the arm of the phonograph, removed the record, and turned the machine off.

"I came for a few of my things I left here." He straightened his tie and smoothed his jacket. "Including these records."

He oozed false charm like a B-movie character.

"My name is Jeffrey Tremaine." He held out his hand.

We shook. New friends. Maybe we'd go out and have a few drinks together, become buddies. He had a firm grip.

"Why did Mildred change your dinner date with her from Thursday to Tuesday?" I asked.

The grin widened. Definitely false teeth.

"You're well informed," he said.

"I found out about it in the garbage," I explained.

"You're the garbage man?" He looked at me from shoes to nose.

"I'm a friend of Sheldon Minck. I'm also a detective."

"Like in the movies? Nick Charles? Philo Vance?" he said with some interest. "I've been in a few movies. Crowd scenes at parties, drink in my hand, standing near a piano where someone was playing Chopin or something, maybe pretending to chat with an actress in an evening gown."

"You're not an actor," I said.

"Hell, no," he answered, folding his hands. "Exactly what you see, a man into his fifth decade, working hard at being charming, reasonably good-looking. I cater to ladies who can afford my tastes. I know a great deal about music, theater, the movie business, style, gossip, and just enough about politics to fake my way through a conversation."

"You and Mildred were close," I concluded.

"When it was essential and as infrequently as I could finesse," he said. "If I understand your innuendo."

"I see," I said.

"Do you? I'm a fading facade, Mr. Peters," he said, moving to sit in what looked like a particularly uncomfortable white chair. He put one knee over the other and steepled his fingers. "I'll be happy to answer your questions under one condition."

"Condition."

"Yes, when I've answered your questions, you allow me to gather my things and walk out the door. I'll leave my key on the table near the door. I doubt if I'm any match for you physically, so I'll simply do what I do best: be cooperative, charming, and sincere."

"The dinner-date change," I reminded him.

"Mildred said she had something to do on Thursday and would be busy for a while after that."

"Busy with what?" I asked.

"She didn't say." Tremaine bounced his fingers together. "I didn't ask. She did add that she was considering buying a new house, possibly in Beverly Hills, and wanted to discuss it."

"Did you?"

"Discuss it? Yes," he said. "Over cocktails at Chasen's. Mildred was exuberant, bursting with self-approbation, confident that she was soon going to be in a position to purchase many things she wanted."

"Like you?"

"Me?" He grinned. "She already had me. I come surprisingly cheaply, and my price has been going down each year. She did say something about adding to my wardrobe. May I gather my things and go now?"

"Mildred the only lady you've been keeping company with?"

"God, no. There are four others at the moment. One is the widow of a rather successful movie director who left her comfortable, but not wealthy enough for full-time companionship."

"You know someone named Leland?" I asked.

"Probably," he said.

"Friend of Mildred's?"

"Leland? No, she never mentioned a Leland to me."

"Give me your address and phone number and you can go. Take whatever is yours. Just show it to me before you go."

He bounded out of the chair, dug into his jacket pocket, and came up with a card he handed to me. It read "Jeffrey Tremaine" in tastefully elegant embossed black script and listed his phone number and address.

While Tremaine scrambled for his possessions, I looked around the house and came to some conclusions. First, the police had not bothered to look around the place. They had Shelly and no reason to spend any more time on the case. Second, Mildred's checkbook in the drawer of her dresser in her pink bedroom on the second floor told me that she had a little over five thousand dollars in the bank. Not bad, but not the stuff you buy houses in Beverly Hills with, unless she was planning to cash in some of the money she had inherited from her parents or was expecting some other sudden pile of cash. Mildred read movie-fan magazines. They were stacked on the table next to her bed. Mildred had gotten rid of all things Shelly. There wasn't an item in the house that bore any resemblance to his name, face, or taste.

"I'm finished," Tremaine called from below.

I went downstairs. He was standing at the door, his arms full.

"Mind opening the door for me?" he asked with a smile.

I looked through the collection in his arms. It included the stack of records, two small paintings of clowns, a photograph of himself on the deck of a boat wearing a captain's hat, and a Whitman's Sampler box. I took the box and opened it. One string of pearls, a woman's watch, two rings, and a bracelet with glittering green stones.

"Gifts from me," he said, his smile so broad and sincere now that I was sure he was working toward a massive headache.

"I thought she was the one who gave you gifts," I said.

"Well . . . "

"Sorry," I said, closing the box and taking it from him.

"It was worth a try, old man," he said with a resigned smile. "I do think I have some payment coming for services rendered."

"Pick one out," I said.

He put down his plunder and selected the bracelet. He put it in his pocket, handed me the front-door key, picked up the bundle again, and said, "The door?"

I opened it and he left. Then I brought the candy box with the jewelry to Mildred's bedroom and put it in the bottom drawer of her dresser.

The phone was ringing when I closed the drawer. I went to the table next to Mildred's bed and picked it up.

"Peters," came the voice of Lawrence Timerjack, "you've disobeyed a direct order to cease and desist."

"I'm not a Pigeon in your army, Larry."

"You are subject to martial law," he said.

"Are you for real, Timerjack?" I asked. "I mean is this all an act, or are you really a nut? I'll give you the benefit of the doubt and call it an act, not a good one considering the small size of your army of Survivors, but an act. Prove me right. Say something that makes sense."

"You have been warned," he said.

I had to give him credit. Only a small quiver of anger came through with his words.

"You threatening me with more peach syrup?" I asked.

"We are talking blood and guts here," he said. "We are talking life and death."

"So you think I should stop trying to find out if someone besides Shelly killed Mildred? So the law can put Shelly away or kill him and you can collect?"

He hung up the phone. He couldn't be far away since he knew I was in the house, but I didn't know how far. I ran downstairs and headed for the back door. I opened it when I heard the front door fly open with a loud crack.

I closed the door behind me and headed for the bushes in front of me looking for a space, a hole, someplace to hide or get through. I found a narrow break between two mulberries and pushed my way through scratching my hands, almost catching a branch in my eye. When I was on the other side, in someone else's yard, I knelt and looked back through the bushes at the back door of the Minck manor.

The two burly friends of Timerjack, Uncas and Chingachgook, stepped out and looked around. Behind them was Deerslayer Anthony. They looked in my direction and didn't see me. They went back into the house.

I moved to the back door of the house behind me and knocked.

After a second knock, a woman opened the door. She was plump, maybe sixty, wearing an apron and a look of surprise.

"May I use your phone?" I asked. "There's been an accident."

She stepped aside and pointed a spatula at the wall behind her. The kitchen smelled like cookies. I nodded my thanks, went to the phone, and called the police.

"There's a break-in at my neighbor's house," I said. "Two men, maybe more. I saw them kick the front door in. I think they had guns. Hurry. They're still there."

I gave them the address and hung up.

"Thanks," I told the woman. "Is it all right if I go out your front door?"

She stood bewildered for an instant, spatula in hand.

"I just finished a batch of chocolate-chip cookies for the USO," she said. "Take a few. You look like you could use them."

There was a stack on the table. I picked up two and she pointed her trusty spatula toward the door near the phone.

"Sorry," I said.

"For what?" she answered. "I sit on my behind half the day listening to soap operas and stand in here the other half making ton after ton of cookies. You've brought some life through my door. Take some cookies for your friends."

She reached for a brown paper bag on a stack near the cookies, filled the bag, and handed it to me.

"Thanks," I said. "Sorry."

"I'll accept the thanks, but not the sorry."

I went through the door, sack of cookies in my hand, found the front door, and went out into the sunlight. I ate a cookie as I walked. I was in no big hurry. I wanted the police to come before I felt it would be safe to go back to my Crosley, which was parked only a few doors down from the Minck house.

The cookies were damned good, and, in spite of the scratches on my face and arms and the possible tears in my jacket, I was feeling good. I seemed to be getting somewhere.

I had a few days left to find out who killed Mildred, save Shelly, and keep Joan Crawford's name out of the papers.

With a little help from some friends, I might be able to do it.

I decided without doubt that chocolate chips were definitely my favorites, beating Mrs. Plaut's teardrop mint and butterscotches by a length and a half.

CHAPTER

11

ON THE RADIO heading back to the Farraday Building, I learned that David Dubinsky, president of the International Ladies' Garment Workers' Union, had union-labeled General George C. Marshall a tool of "a well-organized smear campaign against labor." I also learned that Byron Nelson was favored to win the $12,500 Los Angeles Open, that the Russians were driving deeper into Poland, and another ten Japanese merchant ships had been sunk by United States subs.

It was late in the afternoon when I got back to my office. There was a sign on the door: "Dr. Minck will be indisposed for an as yet undetermined period of time. All calls to him will be taken by an answering service and responded to promptly." It was signed "Violet Gonsenelli, Office Manager."

I used my key and went in, leaving the note in place. I went through the reception area and Shelly's chamber, flicked on the lights in my office, and found a note from Violet on my desk:

Call Miss Crawford as soon as you get in.
I'll be in tomorrow.

I made the call. Crawford answered after five rings with a very wary "Yes?"

"Peters," I said.

"I've had a threatening call," she said. "A man, a few hours ago. He said that if I insisted on telling the police that I saw Dr. Minck kill his wife, I might wind up with a bolt in my heart."

"I think I know who it was," I said.

"That's comforting," she said with a touch of sarcasm. "What can you do about it?"

"Could you recognize the voice if you heard it again?"

"Yes. Faces, voices, words are my profession."

There was something a little stiff in the way she said it. Talk of her profession brought out the Joan Crawford in Joan Crawford.

"Are you making any progress?"

"Some." I took Mildred's crumpled list from my pocket and laid it as flat as I could in front of me.

"Please try to adopt a sense of urgency," she said with a catch of emotion in her voice.

"I am."

"Then try harder," she countered, her voice now determined.

I told her what I had found and said, "You said that Mildred had her hand in her purse when she was shot?"

"Yes."

"I'll call you as soon as I have anything more." Then I hung up.

I called my brother at home. He answered the phone, and I asked if I could stop by.

"I'm taking the boys out for hamburgers," he said. "Becky is here with Lucy. You want to meet us?"

I said I did. He told me where they were going. It wasn't far from Phil's in the valley.

"Hurry up," he said. "We're leaving in a few minutes."

"Phil, what was in Mildred's purse when she died?"

"Her purse?"

"Yeah."

"Keys, a pack of Tareytons, a handkerchief, a wallet. I don't remember what else and, frankly, Toby, I don't give a shit."

"Was there any money in the wallet?" I asked.

"About forty cents. We're leaving."

I met them at the Canyon Diner on Laurel at the foot of the Hollywood Hills in the San Fernando Valley. The Canyon had a neon sign, windows with venetian blinds open and a blackboard by the front door listing the specials of the day. It was the same restaurant my father used to take me and Phil to. He took Phil there right after my mother's funeral when I was a baby. Later, when something was bothering him, something we knew was big but that he wouldn't share with his sons, he took us to the Canyon.

It was dinnertime. The Canyon was reasonably full and noisy, and the smell of grease and onions filled the room and brought back flashes of the past that didn't quite take form.

My father had a favorite booth next to the window where he could look out at the hills and do his best to keep up his end of the conversation about baseball or school problems.

Phil and his boys weren't at that booth. Two men and a woman were talking and eating at my dad's table. My brother and nephews were at the booth in front of it, Phil on one side, his sons across from him.

"Hi," I said, sitting down next to Phil, who moved over just enough to let me in.

Nate and Dave, still in their funeral slacks, white shirts and ties, said, "Hi."

The boys were drinking "famous" Canyon chocolate shakes. They were famous because the Canyon said they were, just like

Napoleon's Grill in Santa Monica claimed it made "the best omelets in the world."

Phil was looking out the window, trying to see what my father had been looking for or at when we were boys.

The waitress came over, and I said, "I'll have a Pepsi. You order your dinner yet?" I asked.

"They ordered," the skinny waitress said giving me a look that said she might not understand that someone had died, but knew that grief was sitting around the table.

"Got liver and onions?" I asked.

"Always," she said. "Anything else?"

I said "no," and she headed back toward the kitchen.

People were talking all around us. Older couples, families, a younger couple at the counter. Music was playing, but softly, a trumpet.

"Harry James," I said. "'I'll Get By.'"

No response other than a slight nod from Nate. No one was looking at me now. The announcer came on and the radio and I thought I caught him saying "Harry James."

"Betty Grable's going to have a baby," I said. "Harry James's wife. Read it in the *Times*."

Phil made a sound that suggested he knew I had said something and that some response might be expected.

"Liver and onions," Nate said, making it clear that he wasn't looking forward to my dinner being served.

"It's great stuff," I said.

"What's it taste like?" asked Nate.

"Chicken," I said.

"You told me salmon tastes like chicken," Nate said.

"Rattlesnake, too. Standard safe answer. Everything tastes like chicken, but chicken, when it's done right, tastes like lobster."

Nate smiled. The smile disappeared fast.

113

"Dad's quitting," said Dave.

"He doesn't want to be a policeman anymore," Nate added.

"I think it's because—" Dave began and trailed off.

"Your mother?" I asked.

Dave shrugged. So did Nate.

"Phil?"

"What?"

His eyes were still focused somewhere in the distance, out the window.

"Kids say you're quitting."

Phil nodded, just enough, if you were watching closely and knew him well, to understand that he was saying yes.

I didn't know what to say, so I nodded, too.

"Remember our father sitting here, looking out the window, never telling us what was going on?" Phil said after a deep sigh.

"Yeah."

"I told myself I wasn't going to do that with any kids I had," said Phil. "They know what I'm thinking. If I go back, I'm going to hurt someone, some bad guy with a bad attitude. I'm going to say to myself, 'Why is this guy alive and Ruth dead?' Then I'm . . . I've got my twenty years in, a pension."

The boys looked at me pleadingly. Phil had no hobbies, no interests other than catching bad guys, trying to clean the streets of Los Angeles with a toothpick. He didn't play golf or tennis. He didn't play poker or bridge. I had a thought. I didn't want to spend too much time considering it. I might change my mind.

"Have any plans?" I asked.

This time he shook his head.

"How about coming in with me?" I asked.

He took his eyes from the not-very-distant hills and turned his bulky body toward me. Our eyes met.

"Come in with you?"

"Peters and Pevsner, Private Investigators. You could get a license in less than a week."

"I'd wind up killing you," he said.

Now, this was a hopeful answer. It meant he was giving the suggestion some consideration.

"Pevsner and Peters? Work with me on the billing."

"Sam Spade Detective Agency," Nate said. "Like on the radio."

"Not someone's name," Dave said. "Something tough you know you can count on to get it done."

"Two Aces Detective Agency," Nate tried.

Phil was still looking at me. We both blinked.

"P & P Detective Agency," Dave said. "Or International Private Investigations, or Reliable Detective Agency . . . "

" . . . or World's Finest," Nate said enthusiastically.

I had no idea what I was offering or what it would mean if Phil agreed. It was clear that the boys liked the idea of their father being a private investigator at least as much as they liked his being a cop. It was clear that they wanted him to be something.

"Think about it," I said.

The waitress brought our food. The boys were both having cheeseburgers and french fries. Phil was having what looked like a chicken sandwich with a side of coleslaw. My liver and onions came with gravy-drenched mashed potatoes.

We ate in silence for a few minutes.

"We should talk about Mom," Nate said around a mouthful of sandwich.

Neither Phil nor Dave responded.

"That what you want to do, Nate?" I asked, cutting my liver.

"Yeah. She's dead, but I don't want to stop talking about her. I'm scared I'll forget her if we make it something we can't talk about."

"Give it a few days," I suggested.

115

"Okay," he said reluctantly. "But we gotta say something about something."

"Phil, why was Mildred's hand in her purse?" I asked.

"Who knows? Maybe she was reaching for the handkerchief," he said.

"Or she had something she was about to give to Shelly, but she didn't get the chance."

"There was nothing in the purse but what I told you. Period."

"Where was the car?" I tried again.

"Whose car?" Phil asked without interest in either my questions or the chicken sandwich.

"Mildred's. You found her keys in her purse. What about the car?"

"No car. We looked. Car was in the driveway of her house."

"Then how did she get to the park?" I asked.

"Red Car, taxi . . . who knows? What's the difference?"

"You said there was no money in her purse," I reminded him.

"Forty cents. Are you suggesting the patrolman who found the body went through Mildred Minck's purse? The cop's name is Andrew Nimowski. Catholic with a conscience. I've known him ten years. His record's cleaner than the Pope's, a lot cleaner."

"Okay, Nimowski didn't take any money from the purse. Then maybe someone drove her to the park."

"Maybe," he agreed indifferently.

"How did she know where Shelly was? Shelly didn't tell her."

"She followed him." Dave's eyes were alive with interest.

"Why?" I asked. "Why not just call him and set up a meeting or go to the office? Why follow him just to surprise him in the park?"

"Is that the way private detectives think?" Nate asked.

"Sometimes." I worked on my liver and onions.

"Has anyone ever followed you?" Dave asked.

"Look out the window, in the parking lot next to the paint

store across the street, but don't stare. A green Ford sedan with dark windows."

"Yeah, so?" asked Nate.

"They're following me."

"Why?" asked Dave with open skepticism.

"Trying to scare me off helping Dr. Minck," I said. "I think one of the people in that car may have been the one who shot at me with a blowgun in the grocery store yesterday."

"Blowgun?" Dave let me know I had gone too far.

But his brother was taken in by the truth.

"What happened?" Nate asked.

"I got soaked in peach syrup."

"You're funny," Nate went back to work on his burger.

"I know," I said. "They want me on the radio, *Can You Top This?*"

"Senator Ford," said Dave.

"Harry Hershfield," Nate added.

"Joe Laurie, Junior," I said.

We all looked at Phil. He was surrounded by a conspiracy of uncle and nephews.

" . . . and Peter Donald," Phil finally said.

"And Uncle Toby," Nate said with a laugh. "Tell us a joke."

"I don't do jokes," I said. "I'm just naturally, spontaneously funny. Like your father."

Both boys smiled now. Dave sputtered. Phil shook his head the way he always did when he thought I was acting like a kid. Then he looked at the green Ford across the street. I saw something in his face, something I had seen before, many times before. He put his hand on my shoulder and gave me a firm shove. I was ready for it. I got up and out of his way. Phil headed for the door.

"Wait here," I told the boys and went after my brother who was already out of the door and stepping into the street with only a nod in either direction to check the traffic.

I ran, but traffic and Phil's head start got him to the green Ford with me about fifteen yards behind him. Phil reached for the door and opened it. I could see the driver. He was one of the two goons, the last of the Mohicans, Uncas and Chingachgook, who had been with Lawrence Timerjack at Mildred's funeral.

Phil reached in and pulled the bigger of the two men out of the driver's seat. The man was at least ten years younger and twenty pounds heavier than my brother, but he was no match for the anger that exploded from Phil.

The passenger-side door opened quickly as Phil, hands clenched into the lapels of the man's jacket, slammed the man against the car.

The second guy, the one with the bushy mustache, came out of the car and hurried around it. He looked determined. I got to the car in time to intercept him. He threw a low left toward my stomach. It was not only low, it was slow. I went back, taking little of the impact.

Phil bounced the man he was holding hard against the car. The man slumped and Phil turned his attention to the guy who had swung at me. Phil went with a short, hard punch to the second man's nose. I could hear the nose break.

Both men were down and Phil stood over them, clenching and unclenching his fists.

"My sons and my brother and I are having dinner," he said. "My wife was buried today. I see garbage like you every day. I don't want to see it today. Get out of here. And stay away from me and my family."

The guy he had bounced against the car started to get up. Phil couldn't help himself. He leveled a left into the man's chest. The guy with the broken nose let out a deep grunt and stepped in. Phil faked a shot at his nose. The man reached up to protect himself. Phil drilled a right to his stomach, and the guy doubled over.

"They can't go away if you keep knocking them down," I said. "Is it okay if I ask them a question?"

"Ask," said Phil as the two rose slowly, both steadying themselves against the car.

"Why are you following me?" I asked.

"Minck," the driver said with a cough. "Timerjack said you might lead us to him."

"He's in the county lockup," I said as they backed away from Phil, whose face was bright red.

"No," said the driver, opening the car door with a shaking hand. "He escaped a few hours ago."

For some reason, this answer got Phil started again, and he reached for the door just as it slammed shut. He looked for the second banana, who was bleeding his way to the passenger side, made a move toward him and changed his mind. Instead, he punched the car door. He made a dent that looked something like a moon crater.

The car sped off, almost hitting a white Carlisle Flower Delivery truck.

Phil was already heading back to the diner. I stood for a second or two trying to turn the goon's words into reality. Shelly escaped? Shelly escaped.

Back in the diner, people pretended they hadn't seen what had happened. Phil went back to the booth, and I slid in next to him.

"That was great," Nate said admiringly.

Dave just looked at his father in awe. Phil had never touched anyone in his family in anger, never, as far as I knew, even raised his voice.

"What do you want for dessert?" Phil asked, reaching for the menu. "I'm having apple pie and ice cream."

"You all right, Dad?" Dave asked softly.

"I'm pretty good now," said Phil. "Hungry."

People were glancing at us.

We all had apple pie and ice cream. Phil insisted on paying the whole bill. I didn't argue. Today was not a good day to argue with Philip Pevsner.

Phil left a good tip for the waitress, who had dropped the check on the table quickly and hurried away.

When we had finished, Phil went to the phone in the corner near the men's room and made a call. We waited outside the diner and, when he joined us, Phil recounted the bizarre story of Sheldon Minck's escape.

CHAPTER

12

SHELLY HAD BEEN scheduled for a meeting with an assistant district attorney and Marty Leib. On the way down, a few doors from the office, Shelly said he had to go to the washroom. The windows in the washrooms were too small to fit through and he was twelve floors up, so the cop with him told Shelly to hurry up.

Shelly, cleaning sweat from his glasses, inside the men's room, found himself staring at a huge, startled Negro woman in a thin black coat and a red beret.

According to the woman, whose husband had been arrested for armed robbery, she had gone through the wrong restroom door. Very wrong. Shelly had threatened her with death, taken her coat and purse after emptying the contents, put on her beret, taken off his glasses, and applied her lipstick. As he did these things, he kept warning the woman not to cause trouble. Then, head down, he walked out of the door and turned away from the cop.

"Gone," Phil said. "The cop went in the men's room when he heard the Negro woman start screaming. He called downstairs from the nearest office to seal off the front door, but it was too late. The cop's been suspended."

"I don't think Shelly is safe on the street," I said.

"Why?" asked Dave.

"I think someone wants him dead, someone named Timerjack," I said to Phil. "Shelly dies and everything goes to the Survivors now that Mildred's gone. The two guys in the Ford want to kill him."

"They want to *kill* Dr. Minck?" Dave asked with great interest.

"Looks that way," I said.

"I'll never forget this day," said Nate.

"Yeah," I said. "It's one of those. I'll call you later, Phil."

My brother said nothing, just nodded, his mind probably with his dead wife. He moved down the sidewalk toward his car with his sons at his side.

I went back to my car trying to imagine Shelly dressed like a woman. I have a pretty good imagination, but not that good. I kept seeing Porky Pig in drag.

Shelly had no money and very little common sense. It was possible he was hitchhiking out of town, which meant he had little chance of anyone giving him a ride and, even if they did, he probably had no idea of where to go or what to do when he got there. It was possible he was hiding somewhere in or near Los Angeles. Since he was born looking guilty, it wouldn't be hard to find him. It was even more possible that, broke, confused and afraid, Shelly would come looking for help, probably from me. I needed a plan.

I got back to Mrs. Plaut's boardinghouse a little before eight. She sensed me coming across the porch and through the door. There was no other explanation since I could see, as she stood there barring the way up the stairs, that she wasn't wearing her hearing aid. The phone was at the top of the stairs. My pockets were filled with nickels I'd picked up at a drugstore on the way. She stood between me and the stairs.

"Have you read my pages?" she asked.

"I have," said. "They are wonderful, a welcome addition to an already fascinating family saga."

I was trying to quote from a recent ad for a new book by Louis Bromfield.

"All well and good," she said. "But we must sit down at the table with tea and peanut-butter cookies and discuss who will be publishing my book and what we will call it now that the story is reaching its conclusion."

I took a few steps toward the stairs. She moved to keep me from going up.

"Tomorrow," I said. "Or the next day."

"I have been thinking of calling it *One Family's Journey Through American History,*" she said.

"I like it," I said. "A little long, but I like it."

I would have liked *A Long Journey to the Electric Chair,* or *Mrs. Plaut's Meanderings,* or *Lost in the Woods. War and Peace* would have been nice too.

She nodded her approval and said, "Tomorrow evening after dinner. I shall placate Jamaica Red with cookies to keep him quiet and tranquil when we talk."

"I'd appreciate that," I said as she stepped aside to let me pass.

I started up the stairs. Behind me Mrs. Plaut called, "You had two telephone messages. Mr. Gunther has them."

I reached the top of the stairs and decided to check with Gunther before I made my calls. I knocked at his door and he called, "Come in."

He was sitting in his easy chair, legs dangling, dressed casually, at least casually for Gunther. Slacks, shirt and tie, vest, but no jacket. He was wearing well-polished black patent-leather shoes and was reading a book.

"Toby"—he removed his glasses—"Sheldon Minck has escaped."

"I know," I said.

"He called here."

"Where is he?"

"That," Gunther sighed, "I do not know, but I know where he will be at ten o'clock tonight, across the street from the Pantages Theatre by the newsstand. He would like you to be there. He was most furtive in his speech."

"There are people who want him dead," I said.

I told Gunther everything that had happened and all I knew and showed him the sheet I had taken from Mildred Minck's bedroom. I also told him what I thought might have happened in Lincoln Park, at least part of it. He agreed.

"Oh," Gunther said. "You had another call. A few hours ago. A Miss Cassin said you should call her as soon as you got in. I'm sorry."

"Okay," I said. "I'll be right back."

I went to the phone, piled my nickels in a small mound on the table and pulled out my notebook. I dialed Joan Crawford's number. It rang four times before she picked it up.

"Yes?" she said.

"It's Toby Peters."

"Well, certainly. I do plan to be there."

"Be . . . is someone there with you?"

"Of course," she said brightly. "Phillip had to go to work late. The children are in bed."

"Does whoever is there have a gun?"

"Not at all," she said. "Yes, the one we talked about earlier. The one in the park."

I heard someone say something in the background, but I couldn't make it out.

"The man in the park? Shelly Minck?"

"That's the one," she said as if I had just won a box of Snickers on *Dr. I.Q.*

"Put him on," I said. "Tell him it's me."

I heard her say, "It's for you," and after a brief pause, "Mr. Peters."

"Toby? You're amazing. How did you find me?"

I could have said, "I just thought of the most stupid place you could go and called there" but I said, instead, "I'm a private detective. What are you doing there, Shelly?"

"I'm trying to convince Joan Crawford that she made a mistake, that she didn't see me kill Mildred. I'm being persuasive."

"You're being stupid," I said. "People are trying to kill you."

"Why?"

"Money, Shel," I said. "I'll explain when I see you. Stay there."

"Can't. The police will come here. I know they will. Her husband will be home. I . . . Did Gunther tell you where to meet me and when?"

"Yes," I said. "But—"

"Toby, just be there."

The next voice I heard was Joan Crawford's.

"I've been humoring him," she said impatiently now. "But I will not perjure myself. I want this man out—"

I heard a door slam somewhere beyond her.

"I think he just left," she said. "I'm going to call the police."

"Probably a good idea, but do me and yourself a favor. Just mention that he came to your house, tell them what he said and did, and forget I called you or you called me."

"All right . . . Mr. Peters, if you aren't going to be able to keep my name out of the news, I'd like to know now, so I can work out something with Warner Brothers."

Having worked for and been fired by Harry Warner himself, I doubted that she'd have an easy time explaining away being a witness to a bizarre murder.

"I'm working on it," I said. "It'll be harder if you call the police and tell them about Shelly coming to your house."

"All right. But please keep that man away from me," she said. "He is a fugitive not only from the law but from a Halloween party for the cosmetically disabled. He's dressed like a woman, or something like a woman. He looks more like a circus clown about to get hit by a pie."

"He's in disguise," I said.

"He is *insane*," she corrected.

She hung up, and I started making calls. I still had more than an hour till I had to meet Shelly across the street from the Pantages, providing he didn't get picked up as the world's ugliest streetwalker before I got there.

On the chance that Shelly didn't show up or did show up for our meeting and then got away from me, I first called Violet at home and asked her to go back to the office and, if Shelly showed up, keep him there and give me a call at Mrs. Plaut's. Then I called Jeremy Butler and asked him to stake out the Minck house and hold onto Shelly if he came there.

"The service for your sister-in-law was good," he said.

"Your poem was perfect."

"Ida Tarbell died, too," he said.

"I'm sorry to hear that. Anything else?"

"Jimmie Foxx may be drafted."

We had wandered into baseball, one of Jeremy's passions. He had once played minor-league ball and was slowly compiling a collection of poems about the game.

"No kidding? How old is he?"

"Thirty-six," said Jeremy. "He's been out of the game for four years. He says he wants to go."

"Keep me posted," I said.

Then I called Martin Leib at his home.

"I have a fool for a client," he said. "But we knew that when we began. If you find him, drag him back to jail and make it look like he's turning himself in."

"How much did that advice just cost Shelly?"

"I'm not feeling generous," Marty said with a sigh. "In my profession, generosity breeds contempt. Twenty dollars. He can afford it. He is probably the wealthiest fugitive in the United States. We are a land of opportunity, Toby."

"We are," I agreed.

I told him everything I had learned and the conclusion I had come to with Gunther.

"Sounds plausible, possible, and reasonable," Marty had said. "It is also unlikely. But the simple possibility gives me something to work with, provided we can get the remarkably elusive Dr. Minck to get his—and I say this with great respect—his fat ass back in jail where he will be reasonably safe."

"I'm working on it," I said. "Time is money."

"Indeed it is," he said. "We've just had a forty-dollar phone call."

"You said twenty."

"I told you I'm not feeling generous."

He hung up.

I went back to Gunther's room and asked him to keep an eye out for Shelly in case he got away from me and headed for Mrs. Plaut's.

"Keep him here if he shows up," I said, having full confidence that the tiny, well-dressed man with the Swiss accent could handle the overweight dentist. Gunther had been a circus performer. He was small but strong. Seeing him subdue Sheldon the Bulbous would have been worth the price of a good dinner.

"I will do so," he said. "But why would he come here? Would not this be one of the places the police might come to look for him?"

"It definitely would," I agreed. "But what Shelly lacks in skill as a dentist equals his total lack of common sense. I'm staking out all the likely places he would go."

One hour later, after massaging my feet, changing my socks, and having a brief conversation with Dash after feeding him half a can of tuna, I headed to the Pantages Theatre on Hollywood Boulevard. The Pantages brought back memories of my ex-wife, Ann. We had gone to the Pantages the week after it opened in 1930, eight months after the market crashed, a crash that took a while to trickle down to us because we had no money invested and none to invest. I was a cop in Burbank. The movie we saw was something with Greta Garbo and Conrad Nagel, or maybe it was Lewis Stone. We had a good time.

That was then. This was now. I parked and walked half a block to the newsstand across the street from the theater.

There was a sign on the lamppost, which asked people to please rent rooms to war-plant workers. The city was filled with people working at Boeing, the shipyards, and dozens of other defense jobs. There weren't enough rooms. I reminded myself to suggest that Mrs. Plaut put an ad in the paper. She had two unoccupied rooms.

"Toby," a voice whispered behind me.

I turned. There stood a prime candidate for the ugliest woman in Los Angeles or the world's worst-dressed transvestite.

"Shelly, you don't look like a woman."

"I don't feel like one," he said.

He was wearing a little blue straw hat with something faintly resembling hair sticking out from under it. His face was made up in what looked like an attempt to frighten any children he might meet and cause adults to cross the street to get away from him.

"Why are you dressed like that?" I asked.

"I'm in disguise."

"You're in costume," I said. "There's a difference."

"We've got to talk," he said urgently, taking my arm.

A young sailor and a blonde chewing gum walked past us, nudging each other and looking in our direction.

"Not on the street," I said. "The Hollywood Roosevelt lobby. Find someplace to get out of those clothes, wash your face, and meet me there in ten minutes."

The Roosevelt was eight blocks away on Hollywood.

"Can't," he said. "I'm wearing a jail uniform under this coat."

Lots of people were looking at us now. We were a better show than whatever might be going on across the street at the Pantages.

"Okay, come on. Walk behind me."

I hurried back to my car, opened the doors and waited till Shelly caught up and climbed into the passenger seat. Then I pulled into traffic. So did the green Ford parked five or six cars behind me. I couldn't see who was driving. I was getting tired and I wondered if the two Mohicans Phil had pummeled had enough fight or determination left in them to come after me.

The light from the Pantages marquee caught the windshield of the Ford behind me, and I saw enough of Lawrence Timerjack's face to know that a new team had taken over.

"That was a dumb thing to do," I said as we drove.

"What?"

"Escaping."

"It wasn't my idea," he said.

"Take off that hat and wig and wipe your face," I said. "I can't talk seriously to a man who looks like a Marie Dressler impersonator."

Shelly took off the hat and made an attempt to clean himself.

"I was minding my business," he said. "I went into the washroom and there she was. Big Negro woman. She said a friend was going to save me, and then she handed me the coat and hat and stuff and started to paint my face. She did it fast and told me to go out the door with my head down and go to the right and down the stairs and . . . I didn't even get a chance to pee or think. I was just . . . I don't know, running. Like Paul Muni in *I Am a Fugitive from a Chain Gang* or John Garfield in that other picture."

"*Dust Be My Destiny*," I said.

"So, are we going to the Roosevelt?" Shelly asked.

"No."

"Why not?"

"Because," I said. "We're being followed by Lawrence Timerjack. If we stop and get out, I think he'll try to kill you."

"Me?" Shelly asked, his voice rising a few octaves to the level of Rise Stevens. "Why?"

"Because you are a rich man, Sheldon," I said as he looked back through the window, squinting in the general direction of the Ford. "And you left a will giving everything you've got to the Survivors if you weren't married to Mildred. Now with Mildred dead and your no-snore gizmo, you're worth a lot of money to Timerjack. But only if you're dead."

Shelly sat back. There wasn't much foot or body room in the Crosley. His sulking options were minimal, but he went for one.

"But I'm a Pigeon," he said.

"You were set up, Shel. The woman in the washroom was sent there by Timerjack to get you out on the street where he could kill you before you change your mind about leaving the Survivors your money."

"Wait," He adjusted his glasses. "You think he killed Mildred?"

"I think there's a good possibility he had her killed so you'd get her money. Then he'd find a way to kill you."

"I don't believe it." Shelly shook his head so violently that his glasses fell off. He reached out to grab them before they reached the windshield and missed by about a foot. I caught them and handed them back to him.

"Lawrence Timerjack is a good man, a hero," Shelly went on. "I'm a Pigeon. We're together. Survivors together."

"You guys have a song?" I asked.

"A song? No, should we?"

"The Boy Scouts have one. So does UCLA. And the U.S. Marines and . . . "

"You're making fun of us," Shelly said seriously.

"Good, you noticed. There's hope for you, Sheldon Minck."

I took a slow left at the next corner, giving Timerjack time to follow and the impression, I hoped, that I hadn't spotted him.

"Maybe I should just change my will," Shelly said. "And you tell him I changed it."

I passed a slow-moving lug of a Chrysler and put a car between Timerjack and me.

"Might just make him mad enough to kill you anyway," I said.

"Oh, I get it," said Shelly with a crazy cackle. "If I don't change my will, he kills me. If I *do* change it, he kills me. What do I do?"

"Go back to jail," I suggested, looking for the delivery alley next to Bullock's.

I looked up at the rearview mirror and stepped on the gas making a sharp right into the alley. Most people who have made a delivery to Bullock's would tell you the alley dead-ended at the loading dock. Most people would tell you there was a passageway just to the right of the loading dock. Most people would tell you a car wouldn't fit down that passageway. Most people didn't reckon with a refrigerator on wheels.

The alley was clear. Timerjack was about twenty yards behind me. Shelly looked out the front window, braced himself, and screamed. I slowed down and drove into the narrow passage, slightly scraping the passenger side of the car. Shelly closed his eyes. There was enough room for me to keep going, but not enough room for Timerjack and the Ford. He stopped just short of the passage.

I was driving slowly, but still fast enough to stay ahead of Timerjack if he came after us on foot. I looked into the rearview mirror and saw three figures in the shadows. The doors of the Ford were open.

Shelly opened his eyes, blinked, then regarded me through his thick glasses.

"We did it," he wept.

Suddenly the rear window of the Crosley—a small patch of glass a little bigger than a license plate—exploded. Something thudded into the dashboard between us. I drove a little faster.

"It's a crossbow bolt," he said.

I glanced down at the piece of metal embedded in my dashboard.

"They tried to kill me with my weapon of choice," he said.

"Weapon of choice?"

"That's what we call it when we pick a weapon for survival," Shelly explained.

We came out on a nearly empty street. I turned right and made a quick left at the first corner. We had lost the Survivors.

"He just tried to kill me," wailed Shelly.

"I don't think so," I said. "I think the woman or the kid got trigger-happy. I don't think Timerjack wants to kill you with a weapon that will lead the police back to him."

"Then . . . ?"

"I think they want to make it look like an accident," I said. "I would. Timerjack's no Quiz Kid, but he's not an idiot, either. Maybe someone else is pulling the strings."

"What strings?"

"Telling Timerjack what to do," I said.

"How does that keep me from getting killed?"

"We find him or her," I said, exhibiting a confidence I didn't feel. "And while we look, I try to get you out of a murder charge and keep you safe."

"Back to jail?" he asked.

"We'll give it a day or two. Now I've got to figure out where to put you."

CHAPTER

13

THERE IS A school of thought that says the best place to hide something or someone is the one place no one would think of looking. The problem is coming up with the one place no one would think of looking. Some say it's a place so obvious that it won't even be considered by whoever is looking. It's been my experience, however, that both the police and the criminals always look in the most obvious places first. They'd be stupid not to.

So, when I was sure the green Ford wasn't behind me, I headed downtown to the Biltmore Hotel on Fifth and Olive. The Biltmore is the city's largest hotel, E-shaped stone and brick, twelve stories high. I've filled in for the regular house detective there and sometimes stood guard in uniform in the Biltmore Art Museum inside the hotel, keeping people from touching the oil paintings and etchings on display. I knew most of the desk clerks.

Shelly waited in the car while I booked a room under the name Wayne Strunk. The desk clerk, a lean one-legged ringer for Jimmy Stewart, showed no suspicion or curiosity. The lobby wasn't full but there were some late-nighters, men and women in military uniform, business types, a few good-looking women with the business types who were laughing too hard to mean it. I took the key, put down twenty dollars in advance against the bill, and went to fetch Shelly, now dressed only in his jail uniform. We went through the back entrance and up the service elevator.

Shelly's lips were moving all the time. I think he was talking to himself. Then, when the elevator stopped, he began talking to me.

"I'm a doomed man," he said.

"We all are," I said, leading the way to Room 434.

"No, I mean, soon," he said. "Is there a radio in the room?"

"Yes." I opened the door. "All the rooms have radios."

"I'll listen to *Amos 'n' Andy* while I write out a new will," he said.

"Seems like a good idea to me, Kingfish," I said leading the way in and turning on he light. "Don't leave the room."

"How can I leave the room? I'm dressed in a blue jail uniform with a number on my back."

"Use room service. When room service comes, be wearing a towel. Sign the tab 'Wayne Strunk.'"

Shelly nodded in bewilderment. There were still traces of smudged makeup on his face.

"And take a shower. I'll bring you a razor and some clothes."

"I've got a change in the office," he said.

"I know. That's where I'm going. What name are you going to sign on the room-service tab?"

"I forget."

"Wayne Strunk. Write it down."

He moved to the night table next to the bed and wrote the name on the pad of paper.

"And don't call anyone," I said.

"Aren't you going to tell me to lock the door?" he asked. "The detective always says, 'Lock the door and keep it locked. Don't let anyone in except me and the room-service guy.'"

"Right," I said. "Lock the door. Keep it locked and don't let anyone in except me and the room-service guy."

"What are you going to do?"

"Try to save your life," I said, and went out the door.

There were some advantages to having Shelly out of jail. No hearing. No arraignment. No need for Joan Crawford to appear in court. I had bought a little time.

My plan was simple. Get Shelly some clothes and a razor. Save Shelly. Stay away from Lawrence Timerjack.

Parking at eleven in front of the Farraday was no problem. Getting to our office with only the night lights and the glow of the three-quarter moon through the skylight was no problem. I walked up slowly, hearing nothing but the echo of my own foot-steps. I used my key, got in, went through the reception room and into Shelly's office, where I turned on the light. His change of clothes was on the left in the closet near the windows. He had a shirt, pants, socks, shoes in need of polish, and an almost-yellow jacket that didn't go with the pants. I gathered what I thought he needed, dropped it on the dental chair, and went to my office to get my spare razor.

When I turned on the light, I found Lawrence Timerjack in the chair behind my desk. He was looking at me with his good eye. His hands were at his sides, his mouth partly open, his forehead dotted by a crossbow bolt protruding from a hole from which blood had dripped down along his nose and over his lips.

I sat in one of the chairs usually reserved for clients and looked at him for a long time before thoughts began to come in no par-ticular order.

How had he gotten in here?

Where were his pals?

Who had killed him and why?

What was he doing in my office?

What was I going to do next?

First thought: Call the police. Second thought: Bad idea. Third thought: Open the window and heave the body out. Fourth thought: The police would identify Timerjack, make the connection to Shelly, and come looking for their escaped suspect, who would now be considered armed with his weapon of choice and extremely dangerous.

I didn't hear the door open behind me, not at first. When I did, I tried to get up and turn. There was no room to jump or hide.

"I heard noises," Jeremy said.

He was wearing a blue robe with a thick blue sash. His almost-bare chest was covered with corkscrew white hair. He looked at Timerjack and then at me. There was no expression in his look, but there was a question in his eyes.

"May I ask?"

"I didn't kill him," I said.

He waited for more.

"And neither did Shelly," I said. "Shelly's been with me. This is Lawrence Timerjack. Until he took a bolt between his eyes, he was the head of Survivors for the Future and probably the one who set Shelly up for Mildred's murder."

"What do you plan to do?"

"Get his body out of here. The building's empty. I'll pull my car up to the back door. I'll take him somewhere."

"You get the car," Jeremy said. "I'll bring the body."

"You don't have to," I said.

"The will is free. Friendship welcomes opportunity."

I grabbed Shelly's clothes, got the Crosley and drove around the back into the alley which was a wild lot of rocks, bricks, abandoned auto parts and broken glass of every shade and sharpness. I knew the way through this minefield.

Getting Timerjack's body into the passenger seat was only a

slight problem—not because Jeremy had trouble with the weight of the corpse, but because of the size of the seat.

"I'll go back upstairs and see if there is anything to clean up," he said.

I drove to Pershing Square and parked on Olive next to a familiar clump of bushes. The street was empty. I hurried around, opened the passenger-side door, and dragged Timerjack's limp body out.

There wasn't anyone near the Beethoven statue when I dragged him through the bushes and looked into the open space around Ludwig. I sat Timerjack on the bench facing the composer, balanced him with arms draped around the back of the bench, and scatted back to my car.

When I got back to the Biltmore, I knocked at the door to Shelly's room.

"Who's there?" he said.

"Mrs. Aimee Semple McPherson," I answered in falsetto.

He opened the door.

"Toby, you've got my clothes."

He was wearing the hotel robe. His face was clean and his hair—what little of it he had—was sticking out in a jumble of small clumps around his ears.

"Aimee Semple McPherson?" I closed the door. "You opened the door for someone pretending to be . . . forget it."

Shelly took off the robe and threw it in the general direction of a chair, missing it by only four or five feet. He stood, rotund and pink in his white boxer shorts and started to put on the clothes I had brought.

"Timerjack's dead," I said when he was dressed and adjusting his glasses.

His right hand was almost through his sleeve. He stopped.

"You killed Timerjack?" he asked with openmouthed awe. "For me?"

"I didn't kill him. The police are going to think you did. Your will? Did you leave everything to Timerjack or to the Survivors?"

"The Survivors," Shelly answered. "But I'm going to change that. I'm going to leave everything to the American Dental Association. They won't try to kill me. They can afford to wait till I'm dead. I'll leave you something, too—not enough to make it worth killing me for."

"Thanks for your vote of confidence."

"I'm hungry," he said.

"Room service. Stay in the room. Your name is . . . "

"Wayne Strunk," he said with pride. "I'm a retired army colonel with a war wound. My wife is waiting for me in Des Moines and my children, Betty and Diane, are both in high school."

"You don't need a story, Shel. The waiter won't ask you for one, just your signature."

"Doesn't hurt to have one ready," he said.

"Have you ever been to Des Moines?"

"No."

"Well maybe the waiter has. Just sign for the food, keep the door locked, and rewrite your will. I'll be back in the morning. There's paper and a pencil inside the table next to the bed."

Before I left, I used the phone to call Gunther and Violet and told them to stop looking for Shelly. I finished by calling Joan Crawford, who answered the phone with a tentative "Yes?"

"We've bought some time," I said. "They police won't need you while they try to find Shelly."

"Is that man really a dentist?" she asked.

"Yes."

"Disgusting. I've been cleaning up after him for hours. If I have to testify against him, I intend to do so with great enthusiasm."

"He's harmless," I said.

"I am not," she answered. "Keep me informed."

"I need you tomorrow," I said.

"Why?"

"Back to Lincoln Park. Same time. I'll pick you up. That okay?"

"I'll see to it that it is. Will you be driving that little car?"

"Only one I've got."

"We'll take a cab," she said and hung up. I hadn't told her about Timerjack. No need.

Mrs. Plaut did not greet me at the boardinghouse this time. The newsbreak on the Blue Network had told me it was almost midnight, though my father's watch said it was about eleven minutes to three on some day at some time in the universe of forgotten dreams. I took off my shoes as soon as I went through the front door. There was no light under Gunther's door when I got upstairs.

I was tired. I went to my room, took off my clothes, made a minimal effort to hang the pants and jacket neatly and threw my underwear and socks into the rear of the closet, where a small pile was forming. I'd have to deal with it soon.

I put on a clean pair of boxers and a white T-shirt and pulled the mattress down on the floor, along with a sheet and my two pillows.

I tried to put things together after I turned off the light and got down on the floor. It was either too complicated or too simple. Too simple meant that Shelly was definitely doomed. So, I had to think "complicated." I fell asleep.

I dreamt of bicycles and Beethoven, crossbows and corpses, at least I think I did. I know they were all on my mind when I had gotten under the sheet committing myself to shaving in the morning and finding a killer.

The door opened with a bang and I looked up, still nearly asleep, at a dark figure that was definitely not Mrs. Plaut.

"Get up."

I recognized the voice.

"What time is it?"

"Get up," Detective John Cawelti ordered.

"Why?"

He turned on the light and looked around my room with a small shake of his head to let me know he didn't think much of my castle.

I didn't think much of John Cawelti, red hair parted down the middle like a Gay Nineties bartender, his face pockmarked and pink, his teeth large and his lips drawn back in a perpetual and insincere smile.

Mrs. Plaut came in pushing her way past Cawelti and jabbing him with the handle of her morning mop.

"What the hell you doing, lady?" he said as she turned to face him.

"I think she's telling you that you're not welcome in her house," I said, sitting up.

The handle of Mrs. Plaut's mop was now aimed like a narrow lance at the neck of the detective.

Cawelti and I had a long, colorful, and not happy history. He had decided long ago that the best way to get back at my brother, who hated him and whom he detested back, was through me. At least, that was the way I think it started. Gradually, over very little time, Detective Cawelti decided that I deserved to be the object of his loathing on my own merits.

"He insinuated himself in," Mrs. Plaut said, eyes fixed on Cawelti who tried to look amused but couldn't help showing respect for the woman and her mop. "He claims to be from Fish and Wildlife. I think it has something to do with that cat you keep sneaking in here."

There was a cop named Sloane behind Cawelti, a big older guy who had no affection for Cawelti. Sloane was there to back him up. Sloane could get the job done.

"Will someone tell me what time it is?"

"Almost seven," said Mrs. Plaut. "I was preparing breakfast, wild-rice oatcakes with syrup, when these two burst in claiming to be from Fish and Wildlife."

"We're the police," Cawelti shouted.

Mrs. Plaut blinked.

"They are," I said.

"Then more's the shame on them for their rude behavior," she said, feinting at Cawelti with her mop. He backed away.

"Get dressed, Peters," Cawelti said. "You're coming in for questioning."

I got up slowly, trying not to let him know that my back was doing its usual morning minutes of aching.

"Why?"

"You were seen last night on Hollywood Boulevard with Sheldon Minck, a fugitive. You drove away with him. You aided the escape of a jail breaker."

"Who said so?" I said, putting on my pants and trying to shake sleep from my eyes.

The sun was just coming up, and I needed a shave, a shower, clean teeth, and at least some coffee, if not one of Mrs. Plaut's special breakfasts.

"A reliable citizen called in," he said.

"Who happened to be on Hollywood Boulevard and recognized Sheldon Minck and me?"

"That's the way it is," Cawelti said. "And I believe him. We checked with the newsdealer whose booth you and Minck were standing in front of. He remembered you."

Dressed the way Shelly had been and given my face, that didn't surprise me.

"Can I shave and—?"

"Just get your shirt, some pants and shoes on," Cawelti said impatiently.

"Like so much doo-doo," said Mrs. Plaut angrily. "I don't

care if you *are* from the Fish and Wildlife Service or the police. Mr. Peelers is going to make himself presentable or you will have to subdue me. And there will be a price to pay for that."

"Listen, lady . . . " Cawelti said between clenched teeth. But he got no further. Mrs. Plaut cracked him over the head with the handle of her broom.

Cawelti grabbed his head and grimaced. Mrs. Plaut raised her mop again. Cawelti stepped toward her with the back of his hand pulled back.

I took a step forward, but Sloane beat me to it. He grabbed Cawelti's arm with one hand and Mrs. Plaut's mop with the other.

"John," he said softly. "He'll smell better washed up, and we'll get the crazy old lady off our back."

Cawelti shook loose and made a face that punctuated his pain. Mrs. Plaut lowered her mop.

"Go shave, brush your teeth, and wash up, but no shower and we're not stopping for breakfast," Cawelti said. "Ed, you check out the bathroom and watch the door."

"Truce?" Sloane asked Mrs. Plaut. She looked at me.

"It's okay," I told her.

"Personally, I think that one"—she nodded at Cawelti—"has nothing to do with Fish or Wildlife *or* the police. I believe he is a wayward drug fiend."

With that, she strode out of the room, and we heard her stamp her way to and down the stairs.

I grabbed my razor, soap and towel and headed past Cawelti and Sloane for the bathroom. I looked back to see Cawelti mouthing something and biting his lower lip while he put his right hand on top of the lump that was surely rising.

"Couldn't happen to a nicer guy," Sloane whispered.

I got ready as quickly as I could. When I came out of the bathroom, Sloane was talking to Gunther, who wore a little green robe and carried a zippered kit with his toiletries.

143

"Gunther," I said. "Two things. Call Marty Leib. Tell him I'm at the Wilshire Station, and see if you can find out if there are papers on the Survivors for the Future and whose name is on them."

"I will," said Gunther.

"Let's go," said Sloane.

On the way out the door, Mrs. Plaut handed me a wild-rice oat-cake in a napkin. It was hot. She glared at Cawelti and said, "I'm going to discuss your behavior with Jamaica Red. He'll have some choice words for you should you ever dare return."

With that, she went back into her apartment and closed the door.

Sloane drove. Cawelti sat in the backseat with me. He kept adjusting his jacket and I watched the sun come up while I finished my wild-rice oatcake.

"I think it has cranberries in it," I said, holding up what was left.

Cawelti pushed my hand away.

He looked out the window and said nothing.

We were at the Wilshire Station before eight. The squad room was just changing shifts, and the cops going off were talking to cops coming on and telling them what was going on and whose turn it was to make coffee.

I knew where we were heading. Cawelti led the way adjusting his jacket as we went into the interrogation room. The room didn't have a two-way mirror, just a small wooden table, three wooden chairs, and freshly painted white walls with a smudge directly across from the door we came through. The smudge was red. Suspects were supposed to think the smudge was blood. It probably was. There was a fat green-gray Los Angeles telephone book on the table. No phone. I took my seat facing the door. Cawelti sat across from me. Sloane stood with his back against the door, arms folded.

"You know a man named Lawrence Timerjack," Cawelti said.

"Is that a question?"

"No. Fact. His people say you went out to his place and threatened him."

"I went there to talk to him about Shelly," I said. "He welcomed me with ax, gun, bow and arrow, and blowgun. What's this got to do with someone saying they saw me with Shelly last night?"

"Timerjack's dead," he said. "Strangled."

"Wasn't much of a survivor, was he?"

"He wasn't strangled," Cawelti said.

"He wasn't?"

"No, I wanted to see how you'd react. He was shot in the face with one of those things from a crossbow."

"And you think—?"

"Minck, with you as an accomplice," Cawelti interrupted.

"Why would Shelly kill Timerjack?" I asked.

"He's nuts."

"I should have known you'd have a good explanation."

"I've got you, Peters." Cawelti adjusted his jacket again. "We start by you telling me where you've got Minck."

"Why don't we start with who called to tell you I was on Hollywood Boulevard last night with Shelly?"

"There's not much left of your nose," he said. "An accident with a telephone book could flatten your face so it looks like the new freeway. Where were you last night?"

"Most of the night, till I went home at midnight, I was in my office working."

"Working on what?"

"A case. We're not really getting anywhere here, John."

"Detective Sergeant Cawelti," he said between clenched teeth.

I checked my watch. It was who-the-hell-knows-when. Marty Leib should be showing up soon. All I had to do was keep fencing with Cawelti.

"Want to know where we found Timerjack?"

"My office," I said.

"No, Pershing Park. That's not far from your office."

"Not far," I agreed. "Sometimes I bring my lunch there and listen to guys on soapboxes warning us about communists, capitalists, government plots to turn us into zombies by putting chemicals in our ice cream, the end of the world, the—"

"What happened to your car?" he asked.

"Nothing," I said.

"Rear window shattered. Hole in the dashboard."

"A crazed seagull," I said.

"You keep looking at the door," Cawelti said. "You think your brother's going to come in and save your ass? He's suspended."

"I've really enjoyed talking to you, John, but I don't think I want to answer any more questions till my lawyer gets here."

Cawelti pushed his chair back and stood up, his hands on the table, his face a foot from mine. He smelled like Double Mint Gum.

"I don't like you, Peters."

"I figured that out from the subtle clues you've been dropping for the past five years," I said.

"You know why?"

"I'm my brother's brother," I said.

"That's part of it. You're smug. You are a smug wiseass son of a bitch who doesn't take anything seriously. It's all nine innings of game time to you. You're an overgrown kid who pretends nothing gets to him. Well, *I'm* going to get to you."

"And Phil?"

"Your brother's building his own tomb," said Cawelti. "Just a few more stones in place and he's buried."

"You have a brother, John?" I asked.

He backed away a few inches.

"You get along with him?"

"My brother died in the last war," he said. "My only brother."

"Sorry," I said.

"I don't give a shit if you're sorry." He slapped his palms on the table. "I want Sheldon Minck back. I want him off the streets, and, as an added bonus, I want you up for charges of aiding and abetting an escaped prisoner to elude the police. In short, Peters, I want you off the streets."

"Why don't we talk about it over a cup of coffee?"

There was a rumbling sound beyond the door and a knock. Sloane stepped back and let Marty Leib in. Marty was wearing a dark sharkskin suit and a yellow-and-red striped tie. He was carrying a briefcase.

"What is my client charged with?" Marty demanded.

Cawelti couldn't ignore Marty. Marty took up too much space, and his bass voice filled any room in which he happened to be planted.

"I haven't decided," Cawelti said.

"Evidence? Reasonable cause? Witnesses?" Marty asked placing his briefcase on the table after pushing the telephone book away.

"Your client was seen with an escaped individual. We have reason to believe he knows where this individual is and—"

"The individual we are talking about is another client of mine, Sheldon Minck, a respected dentist."

"Your two clients, on their own or together, murdered a man last night. That's in addition to Minck killing his wife in the park. For that one, we have an eyewitness."

"In sum," said Marty, "you have no idea of what you are doing."

"Hold on."

"I don't think so." Marty took some sheets of paper clipped together from his briefcase. He handed the sheets to Cawelti who read them.

"We are walking," Marty said. "That copy is for you. Unless you produce a credible eyewitness to my client's association with an escaped criminal, I think I'll have to send a letter to the commissioner claiming harassment and strongly suggesting that, if you pursue this, we will bring suit against you, the police department, the mayor, and possibly the state of California."

"I can hold him here for questioning," Cawelti said.

"Based on what? Nothing. We're leaving here now. Come on, Toby."

I got up and followed Marty, briefcase in hand. Sloane moved out of the way to let us pass.

"Marty," I began as we headed down the steps from the second floor to the lobby of the station.

He held up his left hand and kept walking as he said, "There are two things I don't want to hear from you. I don't want to hear that you know where Dr. Minck is. I don't want to know if you killed Lawrence Timerjack or even know who did it. Clear?"

"Clear," I said.

"You'll have an updated bill in the mail today. Pay it right away, Toby. You need me."

"Thanks," I said.

"You know what I'd like?" he said, still walking.

"A nice tall glass of Ovaltine?" I said.

"No," said Marty. "I'd like Sheldon Minck to turn himself in. If any more people are killed with crossbows, there is no doubt that he will be blamed. I don't want him blamed. I want him victimized."

"Okay," I said. "We get Shelly back in jail, buy a crossbow and kill someone. I've got a redheaded cop in mind."

"Very witty," said Marty, pausing to check his wristwatch. "You keep displaying your wit, and the time clock keeps running."

"I'll shut up," I said.

148

"You have any ideas?"

We were out on the street now, the sun bright, people in a hurry.

"The scene of the crime," I said.

"You read too many detective stories when you were a boy," said Marty, moving to a perfectly polished black Chrysler at the curb. "Killers don't return to the scene of their crime. They stay as far from it as they can. At least, that's always been my advice to clients who may or may not have committed a crime. But do they listen?"

"Do they?"

"Hell, yes. The clock is ticking, Toby."

"Not mine," I said, looking at my father's wristwatch.

"Need a ride?"

"How much will it cost?"

"Nothing. I'm feeling generous." Marty got into the Chrysler and opened the door for me.

On the way back to Mrs. Plaut's, Marty again advised me to tell Shelly to turn himself in. I told him I'd pass on the advice if I saw Shelly.

"He's going to be a rich man, Toby," Marty said. "He'll need a business manager."

"You?"

"None better."

He was probably right. Marty went for your last penny, but he was honest and he was good.

He dropped me at Mrs. Plaut's. The unmarked cop car, which had been following us since we left the front of the Wilshire Station, parked about twenty cars back. There was plenty of room at this hour of the morning.

Mrs. Plaut's door was closed. I didn't bother to tiptoe up the stairs. I knocked at Gunther's door, went in when he answered. He was at his desk, working. He turned toward me and took off his glasses.

"Thanks for calling Marty Leib."

"You are most welcome. On the other matter, the Survivors for the Future. It was not difficult. The founder and sole owner of the organization and all the assets of the organization is James Fenimore Sax. I have been able to find nothing further about Mr. Sax."

"So if Shelly doesn't live long enough to change his will, Sax—whoever he is—gets everything," I said.

"Precisely," said Gunther. "You believe this Sax will try to find Dr. Minck."

"And his new will, if Shelly's written one," I said, plopping into his easy chair. "I'm tired. I'm tired and it's going to be a long day."

"Can I be of assistance?" he asked.

"Probably," I said. "I'll let you know. What are you working on?"

"A technical pamphlet on potential military and industrial uses of magnesium," he said. "It is written in Hungarian, a language designed not for science but for melancholia."

"The poetry of magnesium," I said.

"In a sense," Gunther agreed. "Hungarians—even scientists—have a tendency to think of themselves as poets. It often makes conversing with them a bit depressing."

"James Fenimore Sax," I repeated, standing. "The Pathfinder. The Deerslayer. Natty Bumppo. The survivor."

"You mean James Fenimore Cooper. I've read his works. I find them without poetry."

"He wasn't shooting for poetry," I said. "He was shooting to see how many people he could kill off in as few pages as possible."

"A worthwhile literary endeavor," Gunther said straight-faced. "Though it is not politic, I prefer the German western writer Karl May."

"Got to get to work," I said. "I'll call if I need you. Thanks again."

Gunther tilted his head in acceptance of my thanks, and I went to my room where I discovered what had happened to Mrs. Plaut.

She was sitting on my sofa, hands on her knees.

"You lead a varied life," she said.

"I do indeed," I agreed.

"Who were those men who took you away? They were not from Fish and Wildlife."

"They were not," I agreed, going to my refrigerator for some milk and opening the cabinet over it for some Kix.

"They were the police," she said.

"They were," I confirmed.

"I know why they were here," she said.

"Why?"

"During your work as an exterminator, you poisoned some pond or something."

"Then maybe they were Fish and Wildlife," I said, working on my Kix.

It was at that moment Dash decided to jump from the tree onto my windowsill.

"They were from the F.B. and I.," she said. "They think you are a Nazi saboteur poisoning our water-supply system. It troubles me that people who are responsible for protecting us from the enemy could fail to see that you are a harmless and nearly impoverished American of middle age who ekes out a living killing bugs and editing manuscripts."

"Thanks for your vote of support," I said.

"I shall write a series of letters on your behalf," she said firmly and decisively. "I will write to Harry Hopkins, Cordell Hull, and the president himself."

"Thank you," I said.

She moved to the door, opened it and said, "If that cat gets to

Jamaica Red and slinks away with one feather of any hue, I shall be greatly upset and will not send my letters."

"I'll keep Dash from Jamaica Red," I said.

She left me with Kix, Dash, and a plan for saving Shelly. It wasn't much of a plan. It didn't stand much chance of working. It was probably dangerous. No, it was *definitely* dangerous.

I was, therefore, reasonably happy.

CHAPTER

14

WHEN I GOT to the room at the Biltmore, Shelly was gone. So was my ephemeral happiness. Note the word "ephemeral." It had been in one of Jeremy's poems. I'd asked him what it meant.

"Elusive, ghostlike, difficult to grasp either physically or conceptually, like fog," he had said.

I liked the word. I didn't like Shelly not being in his room at the Biltmore. I liked the note he had left me on the desk even less.

> Toby, I'm all right. I called James Fenimore Sax, the founder of the Survivors. He assured me that the Survivors will protect me. He's a noble man. Believe me. You know I'm a good judge of character. For my courage, he is going to promote me to Pathfinder and hide me till this is all taken care of. Don't worry. I'll call you.
>
> Shelly

The only question for me was how, after Sax got the new will from Shelly—if he had written one—he was going to arrange for Sheldon's accidental death.

I asked the daytime desk clerk, a fixture behind the Biltmore desk since it opened in 1923, if Shelly had made any calls. That was easy to find out. I got the number he called, went to the pay phone booth in the lobby and dialed it.

"To survive is to live and fight another day," the voice said. It was a woman. I guessed it was Helter, the Survivor with the knife.

"Sax," I said, raising my voice about half an octave.

"Who's calling?"

"A friend of Dr. Minck," I said.

"Where can he reach you?" she asked suspiciously.

"I'd like to talk to him now," I said. "It is urgent. Something he would like to know."

"Tell me and I'll tell him," she said.

"Just tell him I have a copy of Sheldon Minck's new will. Dr. Minck will deny having left a signed copy in my hands. That is a precaution I asked him to make. He will deny it vehemently. He knows that if he does not do so, he will not be among the Survivors."

"I know your voice," she said.

I hung up.

Maybe I had bought time. I didn't know how much.

It was getting late. I drove my car to No-Neck Arnie's, two blocks from the Farraday. Arnie and his son, who was just back from the war in the Pacific with a pair of Purple Hearts and a limp, were working on a giant black car. Arnie, Jr. was under the car with his feet showing. Arnie, Sr., he of the no neck, was working under the hood.

The walls of Arnie's shop were covered with colorful war posters. One was covered with little dollar signs and words in black and read "Don't feed black-market greed. Pay no more than ceiling prices." Another had a photograph of a woman with some kind of electrical tool with a long cord. She was working with the tool on a pipe. The words on the poster were "Women in the War. We Can't Win Without Them."

My favorite was with what looked like a red oil drum with wings. Behind the drum were two others, one yellow, and one gray. The poster read: "Keep 'Em Flying Back. Usable DRUMS are like AMMUNITION. Help the Service, the Industry, Yourself." Behind the flying drums trailed the words "Don't drop—keep clean," "Don't strip threads," and "Empty and return fast."

"What kind of car is that?" I asked.

Arnie wiped his greasy hands on his overalls, pushed back his gray Sinclair cap and said it was a Lagonda.

"Can't get parts for these things," he said. "Have to improvise. Arnie, Jr. is making a new driveshaft. Learned to do things like that in the army motor pool, keep jeeps running with rubber bands and prayers. He can make anything run. What can I do for you?"

"Rear window's gone. Big hole in my dashboard," I said.

"Someone throw a rock?"

"Crossbow bolt. Tried to kill Shelly last night."

"I heard he was in jail for killing his wife," said Arnie, returning his gaze to the open mouth of the huge car.

"He escaped," I said.

"Crossbow? Didn't he kill his wife with a crossbow?"

"She was killed with one."

"Junior, you ever hear of anyone using a crossbow to kill someone?"

From under the car came the voice saying, "A Jap on Guam used a sling with sharpened pieces of coconut. Didn't work. A sergeant on Bataan—one of ours—made a bow and arrow when he was separated from his company. Claimed to kill two Japs with handmade arrows. He was a little nuts, though. I didn't believe him. Crossbow? That's nuts."

"That's nuts," repeated No-Neck Arnie, having heard the gospel from his war vet son.

"Nuts or not," I said, "that's what happened. What will it take to fix it?"

"Piece of glass. Fill in the hole with something. Eight bucks. I can have it for you tonight about five or six."

"Got something I can drive till then?"

"Got five bucks?"

I took out a five.

"Little coupe with a rumble seat back there by the door. Runs okay. I'm gonna repaint it when I get a chance and sell it."

"Keys?"

Arnie reached deep into the pocket of his overalls and came up with a jangling handful of keys. He examined them, extracted a pair on a ring, and handed it to me.

"It's filled with gas," he said. "I'll need your coupons and two bucks for gas."

I gave him the two dollars and called out to Junior, "Good to see you back."

"Roger," Jr. answered.

Twenty-one minutes later, I was parked in front of Joan Crawford's house. She answered the door when I rang. She looked more like the movie Crawford, but not exactly. She wore a plain print dress, white with a broad black belt, and her hair was fluffy. She wore enough makeup for a close-up, and she was smoking a cigarette nervously.

"Is it true?" she asked.

"What?"

"That odious little fat man killed someone else last night?"

"Who told you that?"

"An equally odious detective with red hair, bad skin, and bad manners, who had found out—apparently without much difficulty—

that Billie Cassin is Joan Crawford. He wanted to know if Dr. Minck had contacted me."

"Why?"

"He said he thought Dr. Minck might want to kill me to keep me from testifying that I had seen him kill his wife. He was also clearly concerned that that I might change my mind to keep my name out of the newspapers."

"And you told him—?"

"That I hadn't seen Dr. Minck," she said. "And that if I had to testify, I would tell the truth. Mr. Peters, if your dentist wanted to kill me, he could have done so last night. He may be filthy, clumsy, and obnoxiously self-pitying, but he strikes me as no killer. I've learned the hard way how to judge people."

"But you saw him kill his wife?"

She paused and said, "Yes. There was nothing in the newspaper this morning about me, nothing about this second murder."

"The papers are a day behind and the radio is full of war news. We've got a day or so. Ready to go? We're a little late."

She looked past me at the two-door coupe.

"It's an improvement," she said. "I rode in the rumble seat of one like this in *Our Dancing Daughters*. It wasn't comfortable. The road was bumpy, and I had to keep laughing with a bottle in my hand and showing teeth."

"You can ride up front with me," I said.

"Will this take long?"

"Depends."

"On what?"

"Who shows up. What they say and do."

"Cryptic," she said.

She was wearing her sunglasses now, and no hat. She had a great profile, and I was on her favorite side of it.

I parked on the street next to the park, a short walk to the open field where Mildred had died. It was about five minutes before the time of day she had been shot.

"What are we doing back here?" she asked as we stood on the pathway a few feet from where she said she had stood when she witnessed the death of Mildred Minck.

"Waiting."

"For what?" she asked.

"For who. Here he comes."

Scott Kaye, the redheaded school kid, headed toward us on his bicycle. He didn't slow down when he saw us. In fact, he pumped harder.

"Hold it," I called when he was about twenty yards away.

He kept pumping. I moved in front of Joan Crawford and held out my hands for him to stop. He veered to the right onto the grass. The grass was thick. It slowed him down, but didn't stop him. I stepped to my left as he came even with us and shoved him. The bike toppled over, and the kid went sliding on the grass in the general direction of the tennis courts.

"Mr. Peters," Crawford said. "You could have killed the boy."

"What did you do that for?" the kid asked, getting to his knees.

I walked over to him and helped him up. "You weren't going to stop."

"I'm late for school." He looked down at the grass stains on his trousers.

"You may not be going to school today," I said.

"Mr. Peters, I—" Crawford said.

I ignored her.

"When this lady saw the other lady get killed," I said, "she said the dying woman had her purse open and something in her hand."

"So?" he said.

"So you went over to the body while this lady went for the police. Dr. Minck was distraught. You picked up the purse and found something in it."

"No."

"Yes," I said. "You did."

"Okay, I took some money," he said. "She was dead. I could tell. I would have helped her, but I knew she was dead. You're going to arrest me, aren't you?"

"What else did you take from her purse?" I asked.

"Nothing," he insisted.

"One more chance, and then we go in the station to talk about the money you took and what else you found.

"Okay, okay, I found a gun, a little gun. I put it in my pocket. I've still got it. I'll give it back."

He reached for the cloth pack attached to his bike, but I got to it first and unbuckled the strap.

The gun was there. Small. I checked the barrel.

"You clean this?"

"No," he said.

"Then it hasn't been fired."

"I'm really sorry," the kid said. "You gonna let me go?"

"We're not done," I said. "You're the one who found that bolt the other day when we were looking. How did you know where to look?"

"I didn't, just luck."

"One more lie, and I turn you in for theft, illegal possession of a firearm and aiding and abetting a murder."

"I'm only sixteen."

"Then you should be out on your bike again when you're forty."

"A guy came up behind me," the kid said, caving in. "When I was putting the gun in my pocket. He asked me what had happened. I told him about the lady here going for the police. He told me to go. I got out of there fast, but I saw him toss something into the grass."

"The bolt you found?"

"I think so. It was in the right place. The fat guy with the bow thing just stood there."

Three young women pushing baby buggies rolled up the path and looked at us. I smiled. The kid looked down. Joan Crawford showed her profile.

"I'm telling you it is," whispered one of the mothers.

"It's not," said a second.

The third one looked at Crawford and said, "Excuse me. Are you Joan Crawford?"

"Yes," said Crawford.

"Oh, my God," said the first mother. "You are my very favorite. Right next to Bette Davis."

Crawford's smile reeked of painful insincerity. "Thank you."

The three mothers, unable to think of anything more to say, continued their pushing. I turned to the kid.

"Can I go now?"

"What did this man look like?"

He shrugged. "Average, I guess. About your size. Hat, rain coat, mustache."

"What did he do when you left?"

"He was talking to the chubby guy with the crossbow, had his hand on his shoulder. That's all. I swear."

"Did you hear him say anything?"

"Didn't make sense," the kid said. "Something like Dumpo or Dumbo."

"Bumppo?"

"Yeah, I think."

"I've got your address," I said. "We may be calling on you to identify this man."

The kid picked up his bicycle, straightened the twisted handlebars and wheeled the bike back to the path.

"I'm finding a different way to school," he said.

"Makes sense to me," I said.

He looked at Joan Crawford and pedaled off.

"Why was she carrying a gun?" Crawford asked.

"I think she was planning to kill Shelly," I said. "But someone shot her first."

"Self-defense," she said. "I mean, your friend can claim self-defense."

"He didn't know she had a gun," I said. "I talked to him."

Since the kid had confessed that he had taken Mildred's money, I had a pretty good idea of how she had gotten to the park, public transportation, probably a cab.

It was the man in the raincoat I had to find. I had to find him before he arranged an accident for Shelly, if he hadn't done so already. I was pretty sure the name of the man I was looking for was James Fenimore Sax.

"I'll drive you home," I said.

"Where are you going?"

"To a nest of Survivors."

"I'm going, too," she said.

"These people are crazy," I said.

"And this person is angry," she said. "I've dealt with crazy people before. I don't like to be threatened, and I don't like hiding and, most of all, I don't like the possibility of losing this role. I was informed this morning that William Faulkner is working on the script."

I shrugged.

"I don't think it's a good idea."

"I'm sorry, Mr. Peters," she said sweetly. "I don't care what you think about my going with you. You are being paid to keep my involvement in this ridiculous business from being made public. You are not being paid to protect me from harm. I've done a fair job of doing just that for myself for some time. Shall we go?"

"We shall," I said.

The drive to the Survivors camp was quiet, except for the news. We learned that the Soviets had killed 2,000 Nazi soldiers in their drive into the Ukraine. Fritzie Zivic had lost his fight to Jake La Motta by breaking his hand in the first round, which meant I owed Violet another five dollars. Senator Arthur Vandenberg announced that he was supporting General Douglas MacArthur for president, and the State of New York wanted to electrocute Louis "Lepke" Buchalter, who was in federal custody on a dope-peddling sentence.

When we pulled up at the Survivor camp, Lewis, the kid with the blowgun in his pocket, was standing behind the fence with Anthony. Under Anthony's jacket was the outline of a gun tucked into his belt.

I parked and got out. Crawford was out ahead of me walking toward the fence. I caught up with her as she addressed them.

"We would very much like to see Mr. Timerjack," she said with a smile. "It's really very important."

"He's not here," said the kid.

The man with the gun whispered in the boy's ear. The boy nodded and said to Crawford, "You're the one who saw Pigeon Minck kill his wife."

"I am," she said sadly. "A tragedy."

"You're going to testify that you saw him do it?" the kid said.

"I'm afraid so," she said with wide, moist eyes.

"Maybe you *didn't* see it," the kid said.

The older man put his hand on the boy's shoulder, but Lewis shrugged him off.

"Unfortunately," she said, "I did."

"Pigeon Minck can't go to prison," the boy said.

The cabin door opened behind the scratched green Ford parked in front of it, about forty yards away, and Helter, the woman with the knife, came out with the Mohicans Phil had pummeled the day before.

"Maybe this wasn't such a great idea," I whispered to Crawford.

She wasn't having any. She gave me a look that said it's-too-late-now and turned to face Helter who was almost at the fence.

"You're not welcome," Helter said to me.

"I'm sorry," said Crawford. "I don't know your name. Mine is—"

"Joan Crawford," Helter finished. "And you're the one who says she saw Pigeon Minck kill his wife. I hear someone told you you made a mistake."

"Mistakes are possible," Crawford said. She smiled again. "We would like to see Mr. Timerjack."

I didn't know what role she was playing, but I was clearly only a supporting player waiting for my cues.

"Why?" asked Helter.

"To discuss the situation," Crawford said.

"He's not here," Helter said.

"Then, perhaps Mr. Sax is around."

Crawford put her hand to her forehead to shield out the sun and scanned the house and nearby woods.

"Who?"

"James Fenimore Sax," Crawford said.

"We don't have a Survivor with that name," Helter said. "I'll tell Deerslayer Timerjack you were here. If he wants to call you, he knows where you are. We all know where you are."

Two things were clear. They didn't know Timerjack was dead. They had all been told that it would be better for the Survivors if Shelly were on the street. I stepped in.

"You really back each other up," I said.

"Loyalty," said the kid. "Rule One."

"And you think Timerjack wants Pigeon Minck out of jail because he wants to protect him?"

I looked at the goons, whose bruises from the day before were turning a combination of purple and yellow.

"Yes," said Helter. "Out here he can survive. Inside prison . . . "

"He escaped," I said.

This came as no surprise to any of them.

"And those two used that car to try to kill him," I said,

pointing at the Mohicans. "You say you want him to survive and you try to kill him."

Helter looked at the Mohicans. One of them whispered in her ear. What she was hearing didn't make her comfortable.

"You're mistaken," she said to me.

"Timerjack is dead," I threw out.

The kid winced. The woman blinked. Anthony, the guy with the gun under his jacket, started to reach for it. The two bodyguards looked at each other.

"You killed him?" asked Helter taking her very big knife from the sheath on her hip.

"No," I said. "He was shot in the head with the bolt from a crossbow."

"Minck," she said.

"No, he was hiding. My vote goes to James Fenimore Sax," I said.

"No," she said.

"I think your founder may not feel the same loyalty toward you and Mr. Timerjack that you feel for each other," said Crawford.

"I've got to think," Helter said. "I've got to keep alert to every word and footstep."

"Rule Two," said Lewis, whose cheeks were now pinker than ever.

"Well?" I asked.

Helter stood there, knife in hand. Lewis had his blowgun out now, and the craggy man had drawn his pistol.

"I think you both better come in here," Helter said, her eyes moving from side to side as she tried to think. She wasn't a leader.

"You don't want to do anything that will get you in trouble," Crawford said. "Miss—?"

"Martha Helter," the woman said, her thoughts racing, pain in her eyes.

"Martha," Crawford repeated. "That's a beautiful name. It was my mother's name, you know."

"No," said Helter, trying to think. "I need some time to . . . Both of you come in. Anthony, open the fence."

The craggy-faced man tucked his gun away and opened the fence. This wasn't the way I wanted it to go. Once we were inside, it wouldn't take Helter long to realize that she could be facing a kidnapping charge. Then she would have to decide what to do with us. Since survival—hers, not ours—was her creed, I didn't like our odds.

My .38 was in the glove compartment of my Crosley down at No-Neck Arnie's. Even if I had it, I was such a terrible shot that both Crawford and I would probably be dead before I got to pull the trigger, and even if I did get off a shot, the chances of my hitting anyone were long.

Then again, killing Joan Crawford might be a bit more than Helter would be willing to take on on her own. My guess was that she was considering calling James Fenimore Sax, if she had any real idea how to reach him.

The gate was open now. Crawford looked at me.

"I'm telling you Sax killed Timerjack," I said.

"Why?"

"Sax owns the Survivors. Shelly has a will leaving everything to the Survivors. Shelly is about to come into a lot of money, his wife's and a lot from an invention. My guess is Timerjack knew about it, but Sax had decided to kill Pigeon Minck and pocket everything."

Helter shook her head. "You're making it up."

"Damn right," I said. "You have a better story? I'm listening. We're all listening."

"Let's just kill them and bury them in the woods the way the Deerslayer taught us," said Lewis.

"Martha," Crawford said, "do you think I'm a fool? I know you aren't."

"So?"

"We told someone we were coming here," Crawford said. "If

165

we don't call him in half an hour with a code word, he'll be up here fully armed with lots of help and very angry."

"Right," I jumped in. "Ask your boys how angry the man they ran into yesterday can get."

"I need to think this out," Helter said.

"Let's kill them," Lewis repeated.

"Anthony?" Helter asked the craggy man.

"Maybe she's telling the truth," he said with a definite British accent.

"About—?" asked Helter.

"Everything," said Anthony.

"Martha," Crawford said earnestly. "Oh, Martha. If Sax killed Timerjack, who must have been a fine man, his next step might be to kill you and the boy and, well, all of you."

"We're talking about a lot of money," I said.

"How much?" asked Lewis.

"About half a million dollars," I said.

"He's lying." Lewis lifted his blowgun.

Martha Helter reached out and pushed the boy's hand down.

"We'll see for ourselves," she said.

She was still trying to decide what to do with us when a car came speeding up the road and stopped behind us. John Cawelti and Sloane stepped out with two uniformed officers, each carrying a shotgun.

"What the hell is going on?" Cawelti shouted.

"Trespassers," Helter said. "These two demanded that we let them in. We were resisting."

Cawelti looked at the kid with the blowgun, the woman with the knife, Anthony with the gun and the two bruised goons. He wasn't impressed.

"Lawrence Timerjack," Cawelti said, looking at the group of Survivors. "He's been murdered."

"They just told us," said Martha Helter.

Cawelti gave me one of his hardest looks. He was deprived of his moment of surprise.

"We have questions," said Cawelti. "Lots of them—and we've got a search warrant."

He pulled a folded sheet of paper from his pocket and waved it as he walked past Crawford and me through the open gate.

"We've got nothing to hide," said Helter.

"Everyone's got something to hide," said Cawelti. "Right, Peters?"

"Right," I agreed.

"Like what you and my witness are doing here?" Cawelti said.

"Condolence call," I said. "You want us to come in with you?"

"No," said Cawelti. "I want you to get the hell out of here. I want you to tell me where Minck is. I want you to lose your license and do some hard time."

"For what?"

"I don't much care." Cawelti marched toward the cabin with his armed escort behind the group of Survivors.

Back in the car and heading toward the city, I asked, "Your mother's name was Martha?"

"No." Crawford lit a cigarette, her hands shaking.

"That business about having to call someone in half an hour was good," I said. "I almost believed you."

"Thank you," she said nervously. "It's what I do for a living. It's what all actors do, some of us better than others. We lie on film about who we are. And we lie offscreen about who we are."

I drove her home.

A man was standing at the open front door. He was in his thirties, about six-one and one hundred seventy-five pounds. He was wearing slacks, a white T-shirt and thick glasses. He looked like he was in good shape.

We got out of the car, and Crawford introduced me to her husband. "Darling, this is Mr. Peters, the detective I told you about."

We shook hands. He had a handsome face and a firm grip.

"I know you." He studied my face.

"I don't—"

"Pevsner," he said. "Your father had the grocery store in our neighborhood in Glendale."

"Right," I said, still not placing him from anything but some episodes of the *Crime Does Not Pay* short subject films.

"Fred Kormann," he said. "I used to hang around when you played baseball in the park."

I looked at him again. Joan Crawford stood, hands clasped smiling.

"Right, I remember you. Little kid who could run like hell."

"That was me." He turned to Crawford taking her hands in his. "I got the part."

"Wonderful," she said.

"It's called *Ladies Courageous*. Walter Wanger's producing. I play Loretta Young's husband. And I've got a good shot at a part coming up in something called *The Lost Weekend*. I'd get to play Ray Milland's brother."

"We must celebrate," she said, kissing him.

He turned to me and I said, "Congratulations."

"My luck may be changing," he said. "Now let's talk about my wife's."

"I think it might not be a bad idea for you and your kids to take a few days off somewhere where I can reach you."

Crawford stepped between us and looked into my eyes with Crawford determination.

"We are not going to hide," she said. "Phillip can take a few days off and provide all the protection we need. My husband played football at Stanford. The professionals wanted him. He spent most of his youth working in the oil fields in Texas and Oklahoma. He can take care of us."

Terry adjusted his glasses.

"Not against a gun," I said.

"Yes, even against a gun," he said.

"You might lose your job," I said to him.

"I don't think so," he said. "And I've started to make a few dollars with some real estate. We'll be fine."

Crawford clutched her husband's arm with a smile of pride.

"We're in good hands, Mr. Peters," she said. "Don't worry about me. Just find Sax."

"Sax?" asked Terry.

"I'll explain it," she said, leading him through the open door.

I waited till they closed the door before driving to No-Neck Arnie's to give him back his car and get mine. The Crosley's rear window had been replaced, and something had been used to fill in the hole in my dashboard and paint it approximately the same color as the rest of the dashboard.

"Gave it a tune-up," Arnie said, looking into the window of the Ford I'd been driving. "Needed it. Bill, with the gas you used, comes to ten dollars and twelve cents."

"A nice round number," I said.

"Trade secret," said Arnie, cleaning his hands at the sink in the corner with something thick and yellow-green. "Customers don't trust even numbers. They think you've rounded them out to your advantage. You want to give me ten even, I can live with it."

I gave him the cash. Joan Crawford's money was going fast.

"Where's Arnie, Jr.?" I asked.

"Got a sort of date," No-Neck said. "Seeing the widow of a buddy in his outfit. Second time. They have a lot to talk about. He says she's a nice girl. Got a two-year-old little boy. What the hell."

He gave me my car keys.

"See you, Arnie," I said.

"They say the war's gonna be over soon," he said as I opened the door to my car. "But Arnie, Jr. says the Japs won't give up.

They think it's dishonorable. They think we'll kill all the men and rape all the women. A lot of men are going to die, Toby. I'm just glad my boy's out of it."

I waved as I drove out the open door. The car didn't quite hum, but it didn't rattle like a defrosting refrigerator, which was a great improvement over what it had sounded like when I had dropped it off. With luck, no one would try to kill me or one of my passengers for at least a day or two.

CHAPTER

15

VIOLET WAS IN the office when I got there. She was behind her desk in the reception room.

"Zivic lost," she announced.

"I know." I pulled out a five-dollar bill and handed it to her. "Freak accident."

"Freak, smeak, he lost." She put the bill in her purse on the desk. "What's happening?"

"The story is long," I said.

I gave her the short version.

"Joan Crawford," she said. "Could you get me an autographed picture?"

"I'll try. Any calls?"

"Not for you. Appointments for Dr. Minck. Some lawyer who wanted to get a message to him about a contract, something to do with one of those gadgets he's always working on."

"The no-snore," I said.

"That's the one."

"Go on home, Violet."

"Yeah. Is Dr. Minck going to be all right?"

"Sure. Toby Peters is on the job."

She smiled.

"I think he's a little wacky, and I wouldn't ever let him touch my teeth or Rocky's, but I like him," she said.

"So do I."

She grabbed her purse and got up.

"You'll get all the lights and everything."

"Yes," I said.

"Beau Jack's fighting Lulu Costantino—" she began.

"I don't want to hear it. Before you came to work here, one of the few delusions I had was that I knew boxing. You've brightened the office but taken away that delusion. Most of it, anyway. I want to hold on to what little I've got."

"I'll give you good odds," she said. "Very good odds."

"I'll think about it," I said as she walked out of the door clutching her purse.

In my office, I sat in the chair where I had found the body of Lawrence Timerjack. It didn't feel any different.

I needed an idea, a lead, a list. I pulled out my notebook to write down things I could do. Ten minutes later, there was nothing on the list, so I called Mrs. Plaut's. Gunther answered after six or seven rings.

"Hi, Gunther," I said.

"Have you found him?"

"No. Any luck with Sax?"

"There are thirty-seven people named Sax listed in the greater Los Angeles telephone directory. None of them is named James F. There is a Jerome Sax. I took the liberty of calling him. A woman, presumably his wife, said Sergeant Sax was somewhere in Italy with the First Army. I am calling all the people named Sax and asking them if they know a James Sax. One person has a distant cousin in Canada whose name is James Monroe Sax. I shall keep trying. I shall also go to City Hall in the morning and see if, perhaps, there is a birth record for Mr. Sax in Los Angeles County."

"It's worth a try," I said, hearing the outer door open.

"I'll talk to you later."

There was a knock at my door. I told whoever it was to come in. It was Professor Geiger, looking even more like Larry Fine.

"Is this a bad time?" he asked.

"Is this a bad time?" I repeated and really gave the question some thought before I answered, "No worse than any other."

"I would like to help if I can," he said. "I feel somehow responsible for getting Sheldon involved with the Survivors. I was already disillusioned with them when I did it, but I felt that he needed something that would give him a little confidence and a little exercise."

"Don't beat yourself up about it," I said, pointing to the chair across from me as I opened a bill and put it on the pile of bills that had been growing on my desk for the past few weeks. When the pile got high enough, I'd push it into the wastebasket.

"Even without Lawrence Timerjack, they are a dangerous group. A group of fools, but fools can be dangerous."

"I agree," I said. "Did Timerjack ever mention the name James Fenimore Sax to you?"

Geiger turned his eyes upward, touched his chin, and thought.

"James Fenimore Sax," he repeated. "I believe I did hear that name. Once when I was in the meeting room by the lake. Timerjack got a call. It was all 'yes, sir,' 'no, sir,' and several times he did say 'Mr. Sax.' I had the impression Timerjack was getting orders, but I'm not sure. When he got off the phone, he told us all to put on our backpacks for a night in the woods."

"A night in the woods?"

"When there were problems, Lawrence Timerjack liked to

173

spend the night in the cold or heat, fighting mosquitoes and hunting for squirrels, which we had to skin, cook and eat. That, I believe, was the night I decided that if this was survival, I did not choose to be a Survivor."

"You quit."

"And went back to working full time on the Aeolian trafingle. It will definitely replace the theremin."

"You told me."

"I'm sorry." He ran a hand through his wild hair. "I'm starting to forget things. Wait. I remember something else about this Sax."

"What?"

He looked at me with a grin. Then the grin disappeared. "I can't remember."

"Let me know when you do," I said.

Geiger left, and I swiveled around and watched the sun slowly falling in the west. I swiveled again and called Anita's apartment. She answered after one ring.

"Hi," I said. "You eat yet?"

"No. I was giving serious thought to Spam and eggs."

"How about dinner and a movie?" I asked. "My mind needs a rest. Just a quick bite and a short movie."

"My shoes are already off," she said.

"*Princess O'Rourke* with Olivia de Havilland and Robert Cummings," I said. "The one where's she's a princess and wants to marry all-American Bob and President Roosevelt—"

"I know the movie. I'm tired, Toby. Why don't you just come over here for Spam and eggs and we'll listen to *Big Town.*"

"I'm on my way."

There wasn't much I could think of to do to help Shelly, who might already be dead. That was approximately my thought when the phone rang.

"Hello," I said.

"Toby?"

"Where are you, Shel?"

"Safe," he said. "At least I think so."

"Where?"

"At James Fenimore Sax's," he said.

"Is someone there listening?"

"Yes," said Shelly. "I told them I had to call you so you wouldn't worry. Natty Bumppo—Mr. Sax—is going to hide me out till you find who killed Mildred and Lawrence Timerjack."

"Sheldon, my vote for both murders is a man named Sax."

"That's crazy," he said.

"No, Shelly. I think the man in that room with you is the killer. Did you write the new will?"

"Yes," he said. "I hid it somewhere safe. I'm the only one who can find it. But you're wrong about Mr. Sax."

"That's good, Shel," I said, not asking the obvious question which was "If Sax kills you, how is anyone going to find the will?"

"Don't tell Sax where you put the will."

"But Toby—"

"Tell him and you are dead, Sheldon," I said, raising my voice.

"You're wrong. I couldn't stay in that hotel. There were people there looking for me. I could feel them, waited for them to come busting through the door. I couldn't eat. Well, I did eat the roast chicken, the salad, and the rice pudding, but not the baked potatoes. . . . "

"Shel," I said. "Sax."

"I called him and he came right away and got me. I'm safe now, Toby."

There was something odd about the way Shelly was talking. Was Sax standing there with a gun telling him what to say? Why was Sax even letting him call me?

"Can you get away from Sax and get out of there?"

"Why would I want—"

"Get out," I shouted.

"I don't think that'll be possible. I'm being kept in a locked room for my own protection."

"Okay then, where are you, Shel? An address."

"I don't know."

"Something," I said.

He paused.

"There's a dancing fish in the courtyard and a Rexall drugstore around the corner on La Cienega and—"

The phone went dead.

"Shel? Shel?"

No answer. I had a lead. A lousy one, but better than nothing. I also had a question. Why had Sax let Shelly call me?

I called Anita and told her I'd be late for dinner. I wasn't sure how late.

Then I checked the Rexall drugstores and found two on La Cienega. I was about fifteen minutes from the first one.

I got up, turned out the lights, and left the offices. On the way down the stairs, I got an idea of why Sax had let Shelly call me. He wanted me to come looking for Shel.

When I locked the doors and stepped onto the atrium landing, I heard the faint but distinct sound of Professor Geiger strumming on his uke two doors down. I recognized the "Yale Fight Song."

I considered asking someone to help—Jeremy, Gunther, maybe even Phil. But if this was a trap, I didn't want one of them stepping into it with me. I left the Farraday and got into my car, knowing that if I thought about it too much longer, I'd call everyone I could think of—including Violet and Anita—to back me up.

I drove listening to *I Love A Mystery,* episode something of "The Strange Decapitation of Jefferson Monk." Jack, Doc, and Reggie were following a strange man down a dark street. The man was carrying a large leather medical bag. Given the title of the series, I had a pretty good idea of what was inside the bag.

When I saw the drugstore, I turned left and drove slowly looking at the apartment buildings and homes on both sides of the street. No dancing fish in the first block. I got out next to a courtyard building on the next block. I looked around the courtyard for something that might reasonably or unreasonably be called a dancing fish. Nothing. I went back to La Cienega, crossed it, and found what I was looking for five buildings down on my right.

It was a well-lighted two-story courtyard building with a fountain in the middle of a small pond. The fountain was a fish balanced on its tail spitting water out of its mouth. The water made a rainlike sound as it hit the pool of water.

I had taken my .38 out of the glove compartment and felt it resting heavily under my jacket tucked in my belt.

There were sixteen apartments, eight up, eight down. They didn't look very big. Most of them had their lights out. Six didn't. The lack of light didn't mean anything.

I considered knocking at each door and simply asking if they were hiding a fugitive murder suspect. Then, as I stood in front of the spitting fish, I thought I saw something move in a second-floor apartment to my left. When I looked up at the darkened window, I was sure I saw the drape behind it swaying to a stop.

It could have been a curious tenant. It could have been someone expecting me. It could have been someone expecting me and wanting me to see the swaying drape. With no other great ideas, I decided to try the apartment on the second floor.

I went up the concrete stairwell, hand on my gun. I stood in front of the door thinking, "This is really stupid."

Jeremy had once said that he thought I did crazy things like this because they made me feel alive.

"On the point of death, you feel most alive," he had said. "It's like an addiction. The more you do it, the more you need it to make me feel alive."

I didn't buy it. Jeremy had continued, "How many times have you been shot?"

177

"Twice."

"Could either time have been avoided?"

"Maybe. Sure."

"And how many times have you been shot at or threatened with a firearm?"

"Lots," I said. "It's part of the business."

"I know a private investigator in Santa Barbara named Thomas Ross," Jeremy had said. "He writes poetry. He has never been shot or shot at."

"When he's been in the business as long—"

"He has been a private investigator for more than thirty years," said Jeremy. "He is about to retire. He has never been beaten and he has related the only time he has been threatened in a poem which Alice and I published less than a year ago."

"So?" I had asked.

"I don't expect you to change," Jeremy had said. "Understanding is more important to the human psyche. We all die."

"I've noticed."

"But we should all seek an understanding of why we take the roads we choose to tread. The question, Toby, is not 'What is the meaning of Life?' but 'What is the meaning of *my* life?' Have you ever considered that question?"

"No."

"Someday you may wish to," had been Jeremy's reply before going back to scrubbing the Farraday lobby floor.

Now I stood in front of an apartment door having no idea of the meaning of my life or the value of the one I was trying to save. At the moment, I didn't think I wanted to consider the meaning of my life.

I knocked. The door opened immediately and a bright light hit my face blocking out whoever was behind it.

"Don't touch it," came a voice I recognized.

A hand came out of the blinding light, pulled me into the room, and took my gun. It wasn't the first time someone had taken my gun. It wasn't even the fifth or sixth time. I kept getting it taken away. The door closed behind me and someone shoved me back into an armchair, the light still in my face.

Then the light flicked off. All I could see were funny dancing dots of light, particularly one that started on the bottom left and quickly made its way up to the right and into nowhere.

A floor lamp clicked on and I found myself looking at Lewis the Kid and the would-be Amazon Helter. She was holding a plain double-barreled shotgun. It was aimed in my specific direction.

"You want to live?" she asked.

Her hair was pulled back and tied with what looked like a shoelace.

"Where's Pigeon Minck?" I asked.

"She asked you if you want to live," Kid Lewis said, pulling out his blowgun. "You better answer. I can hurt you with this, hurt you real, real bad."

He put something in the channel of his blowgun and aimed it at me like a kid with a peashooter.

"He can," Helter said.

"I believe him," I said. "But I want to know how and where Dr. Minck is before we talk about my future."

"Your future's gonna be short is what," the kid said.

"Lewis," the Helter woman said calmingly. "I'll take care of this." Then to me: "The former Pigeon Minck is alive. He isn't here. If you want to live, we take you to him and you tell him to tell us where the will is. Do that and we find it, and you both live."

"Simple as that?" I asked.

"Simple as that," she said.

"Why?" I asked.

"Why?" the woman answered. "Why what?"

"Why do you want Shelly's will? So Sax can destroy it, kill Shelly, and take the dough while you get insect bites in the woods?"

"We're Survivors," she said. "Natty Bumppo wouldn't betray us."

"What do you want to survive for?" I asked.

"What the hell do you mean? We don't want to die, don't want to become slaves to our government, any government."

"And?" I pushed.

She was irritated and confused.

"What do you mean 'and'? And we stay alive."

"And you get older and then you die," I said. "You eat squirrels and berries and wait for orders. Doesn't sound like much of a meaningful life."

"I'm going to count to three, pull both hammers back, and give you a second before blowing you to hell and eternity."

"Lot of noise," I said. "And you don't get me to talk to Shelly. Sax will say you fouled up."

She hesitated, considered. This wasn't going the way she wanted.

"Then I'll let Lewis hurt you till you agree," she said. "You saw what he can do with a dart."

I remembered the peach can.

"Truth is, I'd really like to kill you," she said. "But I'll settle for watching you in agony."

"You want me dead because you think I killed Timerjack?" I asked and then answered my own question. "I didn't kill him. If Sax told you I did, he lied. *He* killed him."

"Shoot him once, Lewis," she said. "Don't kill him."

I didn't see the dart coming but I felt it hit my left shoulder. It was like a friendly punch followed by unfriendly pain. I reached for the dart. Lewis stepped in and pulled it out while I was still reaching.

"Hurts like sin, doesn't it?" Helter said.

It did. I nodded to let her know that I agreed and was trying to answer with words.

"It's not poison," she said. "You're not dying yet."

I think I managed to hold back a moan. Maybe I didn't.

"You say something?" she said.

I shook my head and then got out a hoarse "Take me to him."

I had decided three things very quickly. I wanted no more damned darts in my body. I didn't want to die while I still had a chance of finding a way to stay alive. I didn't like these people.

"And you'll get him to tell us where he put that new will?" she asked.

I nodded.

"Get our things, Lewis," she said.

The boy moved toward what I assumed was the bedroom door.

"Why didn't you just have me go wherever we're going in the first place?" I asked feeling my arm growing numb.

"Wanted to be sure you were alone," she said.

"Your idea?"

"No, Anthony got it from Natty Bumppo."

"Sax?"

Lewis went through the bedroom door and closed it behind him.

"Yes," she said. "Just be quiet till we get where we're going."

"You think Sax is leveling with you?"

"I said 'be quiet,'" she repeated, holding the shotgun up so I could peer into the darkness of the two barrels.

I was going to say something—I'm not sure what—when the bedroom door exploded and came flying past my head and through the window. I was knocked backward, the chair bottom facing the blast. Helter's shotgun flew in the air and she shot forward, slamming against the front door and dropping to the floor.

Smoke and some fire were coming from the bedroom. In the room I was in, tables were overturned, the lamp was still on but lying on the carpet, the radio had started playing without anyone turning it on. Music. It sounded like Dennis Day singing "It's a Grand Night for Singing." I wasn't sure. My ears were almost blocked shut by the blast.

I rolled out of the armchair and picked up the shotgun. The chair had protected me. I could have felt better, but I was alive. I moved to Helter. She was lying on her side, her back blackened and bloody, her face close to white.

"Lewis," she whispered.

I got up and hobbled to the bedroom, shotgun in my right hand, my left dangling, still numb from the dart. There wasn't anything really identifiable in the room besides Lewis's body, smoke rising from it in a corner. There hadn't been much in the room.

I checked the kid. There wasn't much to check. And went back into the other room. My hearing was coming back a little. I could hear Dennis Day singing "and somewhere a bird who is bound to be heard is throwing his voice at the sky." Through the broken window, I also heard people in the courtyard.

Helter was still on her side looking hopefully at me.

"He's dead." I was kneeling over her.

She closed her eyes in pain, and then the tears came.

"He was your son, wasn't he?" I guessed.

She nodded.

"All I wanted to do, ever wanted to do, was to keep him safe in the world, to survive," she said.

"Sax set us up," I said. "All three of us. He wanted us dead. He wants everyone dead who can identify him or lead the police to him. What do you know about him?"

"Never met him," she sobbed. "Everything came through the Path . . . Timerjack or Anthony."

"Where does he have Shelly?" I asked. "Where were you supposed to take me?"

"Anthony's downstairs," she said with a cough. "He knows. You're sure Lewis is—"

"I'm sure. I'll get an ambulance," I said, going out the front door and moving to the rail. Below me and on the same level, people were standing, looking at me. I scared the hell out of most of them, a blackened monster with a shotgun.

"Someone call the fire department," I shouted. "Tell them there's an injured woman in here."

I went down the concrete steps. No one tried to stop me. The small gathering backed away. Some feeling was starting to return to my left arm and shoulder. Most of it was pain, but some of it was allowing my fingers to move.

I headed for the street. More people had gathered.

"The Japs," cried one woman. "Oh, my God. They're bombing us."

I didn't take the time to correct her.

On the other side of the street was a parked car with its engine running. The driver was Anthony. He looked at me and I looked at him. He started to pull out of the parking spot. I brought the shotgun up with my right hand and a little help from my left. As he pulled into the street, honking to get people who were coming to see what had happened out of the way, I decided not to fire. Too many people and I'm too bad a shot—even with two hands working.

I watched him drive away and shuffled toward my car.

"You all right, mister?" a fat woman with curlers in her hair asked warily.

"Perfect," I said.

I opened the Crosley's door, dropped the shotgun in the backseat, and eased behind the wheel. Then I remembered my gun. My .38 was in that apartment somewhere, probably in Lewis's pocket. I doubted if any of the people who had seen me come out of the explosion could identify me. My face was black, my clothes a smoldering mess. But the gun. I didn't even consider going back for it.

Slowly, painfully, I managed to get the key into the ignition and start the car. I managed to put my left hand on the steering wheel. Feeling was coming back a little faster now, but not fast enough. Shifting gears and steering would have been tough even if I weren't hearing ringing sounds and trying to keep my burning eyes open.

Tough or not, I had to do it. I drove.

CHAPTER

16

"IT'S ME," I said when Anita answered my knock at her apartment door. "Before you open the door, I think you should know I'm not at my best."

"I think I can take—" she began, as she opened the door. Then she stopped and looked at me with more shock than horror.

"Toby, what happened? You look like Daffy Duck in one of those cartoons where Bugs Bunny blows him up."

"Compliments are always welcome," I said.

"I'm sorry," she said. "I didn't mean . . . "

"It's okay," I said raising my right hand about waist high and stepping past her.

"Before you sit on anything, take off your clothes. I'll help you," she said.

It sounded like a good idea. She was wearing a pink robe and pink slippers. They looked warm and normal. She helped me out of what I was wearing.

"I don't think we can salvage any of these," she said. "Except maybe the shoes. No, not even the shoes."

I stood there in my white boxer shorts as she turned me around.

"You're not burned," she said. "Thank God."

I shuffled into the bathroom with her and looked in the mirror. My face and hands were minstrel black. The rest of my body looked almost albino white.

"What happened?" Anita asked again, spotting the wound in my shoulder.

I opened my mouth and she stopped me, saying, "Take a shower. Use the soap and shampoo in the rack."

I nodded dumbly while she ran the water. The room began to steam, and the sound of water reminded me of the spitting fish fountain.

"You okay in there?" she asked.

"Perfect." I stepped into the hot water.

"I'll fix some Spam and eggs," she said. "There's an extra robe on the hook behind the door."

I washed slowly, surprised that my wound didn't hurt more than it did, remembering that the kid who had put the hole there was well beyond pain.

When I finished, Anita was standing outside the shower stall. After I dried myself and put on my shorts, she cleaned the hole in my shoulder with hydrogen peroxide and alcohol, and then dabbed on iodine. I felt no pain. She put a bandage on me and handed me the white robe hanging on the hook behind the door.

"Tell me what happened while we eat," she said.

I did.

She listened carefully. I was hungry, and the more I ate, the more feeling returned to my left arm and shoulder. Most of the feeling was mild pain, but there was also movement as long as I stuck to forks full of Spam and eggs and a cup of coffee.

"Toby," she said. "You think Shelly is . . . all right?"

186

I shrugged.

"Sax hasn't killed him so far. Sax has been applying pressure on Shelly to tell him where the new will is hidden. I can't see Shelly holding up under the threat of pain, let alone the application. Shelly is an expert on pain as long as he's inflicting it on patients. But he seems to be holding up."

"What are you going to do?"

"I'm open to suggestions."

"James Fenimore Sax is not a very common name," she said. "There must be some way to find him."

"If Gunther can't do it, it can't be done. You mind if I sleep here tonight?"

"Sure," she said. "I mean, 'sure,' it's okay."

"How about right now?" I asked.

I slouched out of the kitchen heading for the sofa. She stopped me after three or four steps and steered me into the bedroom.

"I'll take the sofa," I protested.

"We'll both take the bed," she said. "I promise not to compromise you in your sleep, and you look like you could use a shoulder to put your head on."

She was right about that. I knew I should be thinking of some way to save Shelly, but I couldn't think. I let her lead me to the bed. I vaguely remember falling face down on a pillow, having my feet lifted and put down gently on the blanket, and being turned over.

Faint sensation of a warm body alongside of mine. Dreamless sleep and then a tingling of warmth on my eyelids. I opened my eyes, realized where I was, and sat up, my left hand pushing on the bed. A stab of pain hit my shoulder.

Anita wasn't in the bed. I checked the clock on the night table. It was a little after ten-thirty.

I stood up and examined myself for burns or bruises. There were no burns and only a blue and yellow bruise on my chest and the bandage on my shoulder.

I took one small Frankenstein-monster step toward the living room and then another. By the time I reached the door and opened it, I was close to my normal gait.

When I stepped into the living room, I found myself looking at Gunther Wherthman seated in Anita's armchair.

"Anita called me," he explained. "She had to go to work. I have brought you some clothes."

He looked at the sofa in front of me where he had neatly laid out pants, shirt, clean underwear, socks, and a paper bag.

"Your toothbrush and razor are in the bag. I've taken the liberty of placing your wallet in the pocket of your pants."

"Thanks, Gunther," I said.

"Are you all right?" he asked with concern.

"I'm alive. I'm walking, talking. I'm all right."

"The police were at Mrs. Plaut's this morning looking for you," he said.

"Cawelti?"

"The angry one with red hair. Yes."

"I think I know what he wants," I said, picking up the phone on the stand next to the sofa. I made a call I should have made the night before. I called the police and reported that my name was Toby Peters and that my gun had been stolen. I waited while I was connected to a woman who asked me the standard questions: type of gun, serial number of the gun, where I lost it, how long it had been missing.

I got the serial number from the card in my wallet, answered her questions, telling her I had just noticed the gun was missing, that it might have been gone for a few days. She didn't care, just told me to come in and file an official report within twenty-four hours. I hung up.

"I showered last night," I told Gunther. "Just give me a few minutes to shave and get dressed. Been here long?"

"Approximately one hour and twelve minutes," he said, looking at his watch. "I brought something to work on."

He held up the thin book in his hand.

I went back into the bedroom with the paper bag, took its contents to the bathroom, shaved with soap and a fresh Gillette Blue Blade with the sharpest edges ever honed, and brushed my teeth with Dr. Lyon's Tooth Powder. Then I got dressed carefully and looked at myself in the mirror. About normal. Maybe still a little pale.

"What's on your schedule today?" I asked Gunther.

"I am at your disposal."

"Good, I've got to track someone down. Give me a few minutes."

I got back on the phone and struck it lucky by going to the obvious on my first call. A Martha Helter had been admitted to County Hospital the night before. Her condition was stable. She was in the Acute Unit. I asked if she could have visitors and said I was her brother.

"Regular visiting hours are seven to eight in the evening," the woman said. "But a close relative can visit for a brief period if the doctors approve. Let me check."

I held the phone for about a minute before she came back on.

"You can come, but only for a very brief visit. You're her brother?"

"Yes, Robert Biggs. Helter is her married name. I'll be right there."

I hung up and told Gunther where we were going.

"How did you get here?" I asked.

"Taxi."

"How much did it cost?"

"It is of no matter," he said.

"I've got a client." I opened my wallet and saw less in there than I would have liked.

"Four dollars," he said.

I pulled out four and gave them to him.

"Let's go to the hospital," I said. "You drive."

My shoulder was still hurting and the diminutive Crosley was one of the few cars the diminutive Gunther could drive with only a pillow or jacket under him.

We got to the hospital on the 1200 block of North State in about fifteen minutes and parked on the street.

County Hospital is comprised of 123 structures on 56 acres. The Acute Unit is a huge setback building with soaring vertical lines rising twenty stories high. It can be seen from most of the hilly eastern section of the city.

Gunther waited in the car while I went in search of Helter.

At the desk, I told a woman in a blue apron that I was Martha Helter's brother. She looked up the name. There are about 2,500 patients in the hospital on any given day so it took her a little while to find it. A notation by the name said that I was allowed to visit my sister.

She handed me a pass—a white card with the floor and room number and her signature—and I headed for the elevators.

I got off on the sixth floor and went to the nursing station, where a thin woman wearing big glasses and a white uniform told me I could see my sister "for a few minutes."

"Will she be all right?" I asked.

"She'll live." The nurse gave me a reassuring smile.

I went to the room marked on the card and entered. A doctor or orderly was leaning over Helter, something in his hand. I knocked on the inside of the door to get his attention. When he turned, he got mine. I had seen him before. His name was Anthony, Anthony of the craggy face, Anthony the Survivor.

We faced each other. I had a feeling that at my best I might give him enough of a tussle to draw a crowd, but with one working arm and an aching body, I could only fake it.

"James Fenimore Sax?" I asked.

His answer was to throw whatever he was holding at me. I turned my head and it crashed into the door. He rushed at me head down and slammed his shoulder into my stomach. I hit the wall and went down. He ran through the door. I got up, but it was slow going and I knew he would be long gone before I even opened the door.

Instead of going after him, I moved to the bed to check on Helter whose eyes were fluttering, her dry, cracked mouth open.

"He tried . . . " she whispered and then coughed.

"He didn't give you anything, stick you with anything?"

She tried to shake her head and got out, "Going to. You came."

"He killed Lewis," I said. "He was taking a second shot at killing you."

"Why?" she asked, a tear in the corner of one eye.

"You could identify him. You could challenge his right to Shelly's money. He's going to kill Shelly as soon as he gets that new will and tears it up. Where does he have him? Where were you and Lewis and Anthony going to take me last night?"

"Sax's house," she said, her eyes closing.

"Where is it?"

"Don't . . . know," she said. "Water."

"It's near the water?"

"No." She mustered some irritation. "I want some water."

There was a glass of water with a straw on the table next to the bed. I smelled it, tasted a drop on the tip of my finger and held it for her to drink.

"Just a little," I said.

She drank just a little and lay back, eyes closed, exhausted.

"Music," she said.

I couldn't tell if she was asleep, delirious, or trying to tell me something. "Once I heard music on the phone when Lawrence called Sax."

"Music?"

She nodded, said, "Funny music," and fell asleep.

There was a phone next to the water glass. I picked it up and called my brother's house. Ruth's sister answered. I asked for Phil.

"Yeah," said Phil.

"I've got a story to tell you," I said. "You still on suspension?"

"Yeah, and I haven't changed my mind."

"I need your help," I said. "Can Ruth's sister take care of the kids?"

"The boys won't be home from school for about three hours, but Becky can watch them and Lucy after that."

I told him what had happened the night before, told him about my missing gun, and about the attempt to kill Helter. I asked him if he could come and guard her while I looked for Sax.

I expected an argument. I expected a refusal. I got a "Sure."

I told him her room number. He was still a cop and wouldn't have any trouble convincing the staff that he should be there guarding an important witness.

"If it goes on till tomorrow, I can have Steve Seidman spell me," said Phil. "It's his day off." Seidman had been my brother's partner till Phil got demoted.

"Great," I said. "I'll wait till you get here."

"I'll make a call and see what I can find out about your gun," he said and hung up.

I picked up the broken glass from the syringe Anthony had thrown at me and dropped it in the wastebasket.

Helter slept. I stood waiting till the nurse with the glasses came in and told me it was time to leave.

"You can come back tonight at seven," she said. "Regular visiting hour."

I thanked her and went through the door while she held it open. I followed her to the nursing station and started to talk, stall until Phil arrived.

"Are there many male nurses?" I asked her as she went around to the other side of the station and picked up a chart.

"A few," she said. "They say there'll be a lot more when the war ends. Medics."

"You know Dr. Parry?" I asked.

"Emergency room," she said with a slight look of distaste as she adjusted her glasses and wrote something in pencil on the chart.

"He's seen me a couple of times," I said, looking at the elevator.

"I see." She glanced up at my flat nose and obviously injured arm.

"He was a war hero, you know?" I said.

"That's what I've heard."

"Did something to him. The war, I mean."

"I've noticed," she said.

"Makes some men bitter, you know?"

"I know," she said, putting down the chart and picking up another. "I have to make my rounds now, Mr. Biggs."

She had a clipboard in her right hand as she came back around the nurses' station.

I was being told nicely to get the hell off her floor. I tried to think of something else to say.

"One more thing," I said.

She paused, grasped the clipboard to her small breasts and looked at the supposedly distraught brother of one of her patients with clear signs of impatience.

"And that is?" she asked.

Before I had to come up with something, the elevator door opened and Phil stepped out, slacks, white shirt, blue zippered jacket with the hint of a holster bulging under his left arm.

He ignored me and addressed the nurse.

"I'm Detective Lieutenant Pevsner," he said showing his badge. "I'm here to watch a Miss Martha Helter. She's a material witness in a murder, and we don't want her trying to get away."

"She's in no condition to go anywhere," the nurse said.

Phil sighed and said, "I'm sure you're right, but this isn't my idea. My captain sent me, and so here I am."

"Good-bye," I told the nurse. "I'll be back at seven."

I heard Phil ask the nurse for a chair as the elevator doors closed.

"I saw your brother enter the hospital," Gunther said as I got back in the car.

"I called him. Sax tried to kill Helter. Phil is going to watch her."

"Then," said Gunther, "where shall we go?"

It was a good question. We should go where Shelly was, if he was still alive—save him, nail Sax, save Joan Crawford's reputation, and go back to Mrs. Plaut's, where I could get undressed and lie on my mattress for a week or two.

"Wilshire Police Station," I said.

Gunther looked at me, pursed his lips, and decided to say, "Is that wise?"

"Can't go back to Mrs. Plaut's. They'll be watching for me there. Cops and probably Sax. Same for my office. Let's go surprise Cawelti."

"If you think that best." Gunther started the car and made it clear that he did not agree.

At the Wilshire Station, I waved at Corso at the desk before Gunther and I went up the stairs to the squad room. Cawelti was leaning over a desk, his face about six inches from the detective sitting behind it. The detective's name was Bywaters. He had about a dozen years in, and Cawelti wasn't going to break through Bywaters's bored expression.

The room was reasonably full. Typewriters clattering, people talking, a woman weeping, a skinny Mexican-looking guy in a zoot suit sitting on the wooden waiting bench swaying from side to side with a smile on his face, eyes closed, singing something in Spanish. A short, heavy Negro woman on the singing Mexican's right clutched her bulging brown shopping bag and moved as far over as she could to avoid contact with him.

Cawelti looked our way, stopped in mid-expletive, caught the look of surprise and smiled.

Gunther was at least slightly out of place in most locations, but not here. People came into the squad room in all sizes, shapes, colors, and attitudes. He wasn't even worth a second glance by people caught up in their own problems and the legal system.

"Been looking for you," said Cawelti as he approached me, voice raised over the noise level. He ignored Gunther.

"I've been busy," I said.

"I know. Come with me."

I didn't like his confident tone. I didn't like his smile. But then again, I didn't like him when he was being his usual boiling self, either.

He moved around the desks and went to my brother's office, opening it for us. We stepped in and he closed the door decisively.

The desk was clear. The walls were clear. A chair behind the desk. Two in front of it. There was a wooden crate near the door with a colorful sticker on the side with the painting of a dark-haired white-toothed red-lipped girl in a turban. She was holding an orange. Under her picture were the words "Florida Tender, Juicy Oranges from the Gibson Palmetto Groves."

There were no oranges in the crate now, just a pile of papers, some small cardboard boxes, framed awards, and a photograph of Phil, his three kids, and Ruth looking up at me.

"Have a seat," Cawelti said, brushing back his hair with both hands.

He got behind the desk and waited for Gunther and me to sit.

"This your office now?" I asked.

"Mine? No," said Cawelti, looking around. "But, with Phil officially resigning effective the end of the month, I'd say the odds were good that I'll be moving in here."

"I wouldn't do it till Phil's officially gone," I said.

He held up both hands. "Wouldn't think of it. I didn't pack up his stuff. Seidman came in and did it. You want to take the box with you?"

"No room in my car," I said. "I'll let Phil pick it up. He might want to say good-bye to you."

"We're going to give him a party." Cawelti grinned, his hands folded on the desk. "I'm not sure when it will be, but I'll be sure to be here for it, even chipped in a five for a retirement present."

"You're a saint," I said.

"You want some coffee?" he asked me.

"No."

"Little guy want some?"

"I don't know, John," I said. "Do you?"

He unfolded his hands and leaned back. I wasn't going to get through to him. He had a rabbit or a snake in his pocket. He would let it out soon.

"Chair's not comfortable," he said. "A hard ass on a hard chair was all right for Phil, but I think the next person in here will bring his own chair."

"I heard the commissioner is thinking of promoting Connie Jacobian from undercover to detective," I said. "Heard the commissioner and mayor thought they could make some big publicity points by appointing the first female detective captain in a major American city."

Cawelti's smile dropped. The old look I had come to know and loathe came back for an instant and then disappeared.

"You're yakking, Peters," he said.

I shrugged.

"Got something for you," he said reaching into the desk drawer and coming out with a gun. I recognized it. "Yours. Serial number checks with your registration. Know where we found it?"

"I reported it stolen," I said.

Gunther interrupted, "I think I'd like a cup of coffee."

"Wait." Cawelti didn't remove his eyes from my face. "You reported it stolen about an hour ago. It was found last night at a murder scene."

"I didn't notice it was gone till this morning. I called as soon as

I checked my glove compartment and found it missing. Did some-one get shot with it?"

"No," he said. "But a kid died, the kid from the Survivors com-pound, Lewis Helter. Remember him? Blowgun."

"Sorry to hear that," I said.

"His mother's in County Hospital," he said. "Burns, concus-sion. Might die. Remember her, too?"

"His mother?"

"Martha Helter," Cawelti said. "How could you forget your own sister, Mr. Biggs?"

He had me. The explanation was simple. The nursing station had been told to report on any visitors. The nurse with the glasses had probably called in my description before I had even left the hospital. It's not hard to describe me. Flat nose, a few scars and a face that wouldn't get me any leading-man roles.

I waited for him to say something about Phil being at the hos-pital. Since Phil was a cop and showed his identification, the nurse had probably not considered him to be someone whose presence needed to be reported. I didn't enlighten Cawelti.

"No answer?" said Cawelti with obvious joy. "Then how about this? In the bombing that killed the kid and may yet kill the Helter woman, a man escaped, a man with a shotgun and a limp left arm. Any idea of who that might be?"

"A Nazi saboteur," I said.

"An escapee from the state mental facility," said Gunther.

"John Wayne," I guessed.

"Hermann Goering," said Gunther.

I was watching Cawelti. His face was almost the color of his hair. I knew I couldn't have been identified with certainty by any of the witnesses from last night. I had been covered in thick soot.

"How's your arm?" Cawelti asked.

"Which one?"

"The left arm," he said. "Let's see you lift it over your head."

I grinned and threw my arm up toward the ceiling. It hurt like hell and I fought to keep from throwing up or passing out. I kept grinning and flexed my fingers.

"Feels fine," I said.

"Take off your shirt and jacket," Cawelti said.

I hesitated. Gunther said, "County police guidelines and Los Angeles Police Department regulations concur that without a warrant, the police cannot conduct an examination of a citizen unless there is sufficient cause to believe that he might be illegally armed. You will require a writ to get Mr. Peters to remove his shirt unless, of course, you wish to charge him with a crime."

"Okay," said Cawelti. "I'll charge him, you little smart-ass son of a bitch."

"With what?" asked Gunther.

"Obstructing justice. Resisting arrest. Suspicion of murder. Leaving the scene of a crime," said Cawelti.

"The department has been sued twice in the last eight months for dubious arrests of citizens," said Gunther. "In both instances, the cases were settled out of court with cash compensation and disciplinary action against the arresting officer."

"How would you like to be stepped on like a bug?" Cawelti said, getting up from behind the desk.

"I would like very much for you to make the attempt in front of a witness," said Gunther calmly.

"Am I under arrest, John?" I asked.

He hated when I called him "John" instead of "Detective Cawelti" or even just "Cawelti." It was one of the small pleasures I had when I was with him.

"Get the hell out," he said, sitting again.

"My gun." I rose, along with Gunther.

"That stays. We're still checking it out. You're still a suspect and you're staying one. And if you were thinking of leaving town, please, please do, so I can track down your ass and pen you like a baboon in Griffith Park Zoo."

"It's always good to talk to you, John," I said.

"Wait," he said as Gunther reached for the door. "Minck."

"I'll be straight with you, John," I said. "I'm looking for him. I think someone helped break him out of jail to kill him, the someone who really killed Mildred Minck."

"Bullshit. Minck killed her. We've got a witness."

"I'll give you a name," I said.

"A name?"

"The person who got Shelly out of jail, the one who plans to kill him. Sax, James Fenimore Sax, founder of the Survivors for the Future. I think he's a white-haired guy with a craggy tan face who uses the name 'Anthony.'"

"Anthony what?" asked Cawelti.

"Don't know," I said. "I'll tell you when I do."

"Then Minck is dead?"

"I don't think so," I said. "He's got something Sax wants, and as long as Shelly doesn't tell him where it is, Shelly stays alive."

"What the hell are you talking about, Peters?" Cawelti said, rounding the desk and taking a step toward us.

"Hope," I said.

Gunther and I went through the door into the squad room, expecting the door behind us to open, but it didn't. We said nothing till we got back on the street.

"All that stuff about police guidelines and lawsuits," I said.

"I took some liberties with the stipulations of the law and the nature of certain complaints against the police," he said with dignity as we got to the Crosley.

"You lied," I said.

"Convincingly, I believe."

"Very," I said.

"How is your arm?"

We got in the car.

"Hurts," I said.

"I shall drive you to Dr. Hodgdon's," he said. "There may have been some slow-working poison in that dart. The pygmies of Guam have an extract from the venom of the brown tree snake that can cause pain and very gradual paralysis."

We were in traffic now.

"I appreciate the words of comfort," I said.

"Reality must accompany comfort if the solace is to be of meaningful value," he said. "Shall we stop for coffee and something to eat on the way?"

"Think I'll live that long?" I asked.

"If it is the toxic venom of which I spoke, it will take some time before the effects are irreversible."

"I'm comforted," I said. "I'm in pain. I'm comforted and I'm hungry."

We stopped at a bustling deli on Melrose and had the fifty-cent luncheon special. The coffee was good.

CHAPTER

DOC HODGDON WAS eighty. He had retired about ten years ago to read, play handball at the Downtown YMCA, where he regularly beat me, do some research, and write a book. The working title of the book was *Watch What You Eat*. The subtitle was *It Could Be Fatal*. He still saw an occasional patient in his office at home and had sewn me together from time to time.

"Infected," he pronounced as I sat on his examining table. He inspected and touched the skin around my wound. "Not poisoned. This happened last night?"

"Before midnight," I said.

"Definitely not poison," he said, changing the bandage on my shoulder. "Whoever patched you up did a good job."

"Her name's Anita," I said.

"Nurse?"

"Works at a drugstore lunch counter."

"She's in the wrong line," he said. "Never saw a dart wound before. Interesting."

"Very," I said.

"I have seen one," Gunther said. "In the circus in Austria long before the war. Intentionally inflicted in that instance also. Caused the loss of the eye of Herman Salthoffer, an aerialist. He wore a patch after that and claimed a war wound so he could collect a pension."

"Takes all kinds," said Doc Hodgdon, helping me on with my shirt. "You won't be playing handball for a while. Try not to use that arm."

"I'll try," I said. "What do I owe you?"

"Nothing, Toby," he said. "Unless you can deliver a late life of relatively good health, quiet tranquillity, and the assurance that I will finish my book."

"You've got it," I said.

Back in the car, I told Gunther I'd drop him at Mrs. Plaut's, check for messages and head for my office.

"Shelly might get a chance to call me again," I said.

"And if not?" Gunther asked.

"Then Sax might try to kill me again."

"And that is what you wish?"

"Don't think I have much choice, and if I'm lucky I'll get him."

"A trap?" Gunther said enthusiastically.

"As soon as I figure one out."

"May I ponder it?"

"Be my guest."

When we got to Mrs. Plaut's, she said there had been no phone calls, but that didn't mean she was right. Without her hearing aid, a blockbuster could have dropped three blocks away on Hollywood Boulevard and she wouldn't have heard it.

"The police were here," she said. "The disagreeable man with red hair."

"I'm sorry," I said.

"I think his teeth are false," she said.

"You may well be right," I agreed.

Gunther nodded to indicate that he, too, agreed.

"Mrs. Plaut, your late husband's pistol," I said. "You still have it?"

"The Buntline Special? Of course. It was one of his treasures. He once had the honor when he was a boy of firing it at Geronimo. Of course that was after Geronimo was tamed, but the mister was young and impetuous and carried his grudges lovingly."

"He missed Geronimo," I said.

"How did you know that?" she asked.

"Because Geronimo died of old age," I said.

"Indeed," she said pensively, "were not my mister not but a bit more than a child, I think he would have been chastised severely, his weapon removed and his liberty curtailed."

"But you have it?"

She had shown it to me once, a long-barreled antique that she kept oiled in a drawer in her sitting room.

"Loaded and always ready for the descendants of Geronimo to seek me out for revenge. The mister warned me that Indians either forgot attempts on their lives immediately or held their hurts in the family forever."

"Interesting," I said. "You think I might borrow the gun?"

She cocked her head to one side. "You mean to shoot some-thing with it?"

"It might come to that." I didn't mention that the most likely person to be shot when I had a gun in my possession was me.

"You're after large vermin?" she asked, and I realized she was talking to her boarder Tony Peelers in his capacity as exterminator.

"Very large," I said.

"Badger, coyotes?"

"Maybe both, maybe something bigger."

"Then the mister's gun is just the ticket. I'll get it and a box of bullets."

While she went for the gun, Gunther said, "Toby, recall what Dr. Hodgdon said about your arm. Perhaps I should accompany you?"

"I'll be fine, Gunther. Thanks."

I pictured Gunther holding the gun, which was probably as long as one of his arms and twice as heavy.

Mrs. Plaut returned with the weapon and handed it to me. The barrel was about a foot long.

"Fully loaded and ready," she said. "Single action. There are some that say this gun never existed, that Ned Buntline, the famous writer, never gave one to Wyatt Earp. Well, it may be that he did not give one to Marshal Earp, but in your hands is the proof of its existence."

Then she handed me the box of bullets. The box was red and white, and on it was written in ink "Purchased this day of May 10, 1881." I put the bullets in my pocket and considered how to hide the gun.

"Wait," said Gunter, hurrying up the stairs to his room.

"Keep it clean. Shoot it straight and if the creature you kill is of edible ilk, bring him to me."

"I will," I said, wondering if badger and coyote were edible in Mrs. Plaut's culinary world. I didn't choose to think about humans.

Gunther came back down the stairs carrying his briefcase.

"It may fit in this," he said, handing it to me.

I slipped the gun in. It just barely fit at an angle. I snapped the buckle.

"You look like an editor now," Mrs. Plaut said.

"I'm a man of many professions," I said. "Thanks for the Buntline."

"No notches in the handle if you kill anything," she said. "The mister was most particular about that. He would say, 'People who notch their guns when they kill are fools. They announce their deeds and attract enemies.'"

"I'll remember that," I said. "I've got a call to make. I'll be right back down."

Gunther and Mrs. Plaut stood talking while I went up the stairs, briefcase in my right hand, moving slowly to appease the pain in my shoulder.

At the top of the stairs, I put down the briefcase and went into my pocket for change, found it, and pulled out my notebook.

Phil Terry answered the phone.

"It's Toby Peters. Is your wife there?"

"No. She's at Warner Brothers. Script reading with Curtiz. She wasn't looking forward to it."

"I'll call back later," I said. "Tell her I think I've got things taken care of. She'll understand."

"I hope the police don't cause a problem at the studio," he said. "There are always reporters around."

"Police?"

"Policeman called a little while ago and asked to talk to Joan. I told him she was at the studio."

"What did the policeman sound like?" I asked.

"Funny you should ask. British accent. Not much of one, but I've done British and . . . I didn't know there were Englishmen on the Los Angeles Police Department."

"Takes all kinds," I said. "He was driving a green Ford?"

"Green Ford. Yeah, now that you mention it."

I hung up.

Anthony—or, if I was right, Sax—had a British accent. I called the front gate at Warner Brothers. Claude Herman answered. Claude had been at Warner working the gate long before I went to Warner for my five years there as a security guard.

"Claude, it's Toby, Toby Peters. Has a cop come there looking for Joan Crawford?"

"A few minutes ago," he said.

"British accent?"

"Maybe, now that you mention it. Showed me his badge."

"He wasn't a cop."

"Looked like one, had the badge." Claude, who was nearing retirement, said this defensively.

"Send security to find him," I said. "He's after Joan Crawford."

"Well . . . his credentials looked good, Toby. It's *you* who's on the permanent list of people not welcome on the lot," he reminded me.

Harry Warner himself had put me on the list and fired me when I broke the nose of a B-western star who was mauling a very young would-be starlet. The cowboy's nose couldn't be covered with enough makeup to keep shooting.

A kid editor I knew named Don Siegel, who had just started to do second-unit work, had suggested they write in a scene in which the cowboy gets his nose broken.

"No one wants to see him with a broken nose," Harry Warner had said.

Shooting had been delayed three weeks. My firing was immediate. That's what started me in the private detective business.

"Claude . . . "

"Sorry, Toby. If I call for a pickup on a cop and have to tell them it was your idea, I could lose my pension. You might—"

I didn't stop to listen to what I might do. I considered calling the police, but didn't think I'd get a much better reception there.

If I strained the Crosley and was lucky enough not to get stopped by a cop—which was likely, since the Crosley couldn't do more than a few miles over any local speed limit—and if I didn't get caught running any red lights, I could make it to Burbank in twenty minutes. Maybe. I ran down the stairs with the briefcase, ignoring the pain in my shoulder.

"Got to go," I said, running to the door.

"Take care of yourself, Toby," Gunther said. "And call me should you have the need."

"I will," I said.

I made it to the Warner gate in twenty-five minutes. There was a car ahead of me. Allan Jenkins was leaning out of the window smiling and talking to Claude, who was laughing.

I hit my horn. Jenkins turned to give me a dirty look and recognized me. He had been on the Warner lot as a character actor almost as long as Claude had been a security guard. He pulled into the lot, and I pulled up to the open window of the guard box.

Claude was a bulky, ruddy-faced sixty-year-old with a tight uniform and cap and a frown.

"Can't let you in, Toby," he said.

"That guy with the British accent. Has he come out?"

"No."

"He may be trying to kill Joan Crawford right now," I said. "You've got to let me in."

He shook his head and I took a deep breath.

"Okay," I said. "Any idea where she is? We can call her."

"Stage Five," he said, "but I'm not—"

I stepped on the gas. The Crosley clattered forward and started to pick up speed. I could hear Claude calling my name plaintively behind me. I'd explain to whoever I had to explain to that I had run the gate.

I didn't have a lot of time. I was sure Claude was already calling the security office. However, having worked in it, I knew I could get to Stage Five before anyone from security made it.

I went past three girls wearing orange tights and peacock feathers circling out from their rear ends. The feathers fluttered as they stepped back out of my way.

Stage Five was to my right. I drove to it, grabbed the briefcase and got out of the Crosley as fast as I could. I was right outside the door. The red light wasn't on. I went through the door and looked across the huge empty stage. There was a table and six chairs and a rack of costumes. Michael Curtiz, who had just been assigned *Casablanca* when I was fired, was standing with a clipboard talking to a girl in a gray suit who was taking notes. He was about my height, had a receding hairline, and was wearing a frown.

"The next time I want some son of a bitch to do something," he was telling the girl in his thick Hungarian accent, "I'll do it myself."

They looked at me as I hurried toward them, the Buntline jiggling in the briefcase I carried.

"Joan Crawford?" I asked.

Curtiz looked at me and said, "Don't talk to me while I'm interrupting."

"Joan Crawford," I repeated.

Curtiz gave me his best withering look and said, "You are that madman who was fired for hitting that cowboy. I remember you."

"Is Joan Crawford here?" I repeated.

"She was," said the girl. "A policeman came and asked her to go with him."

"He had to wait till we finished our reading," said Curtiz. "Policeman or no policeman."

"How long ago did they leave?" I asked.

"Just a few minutes ago," the girl said.

I ran back across the stage toward the door and got out just as a trio of uniformed security guards came running down the wide space between the soundstages. I got in my car and drove hard toward the gate.

Claude was standing outside his guard box, cap in his hand, looking nervous. I pulled up next to him.

"Which way did the cop go?" I asked. "He just pulled out of here with Joan Crawford, right?"

"Toby, I—"

"He may be taking her someplace to kill her," I said.

"Oh crap," said Claude, seeing his pension flying.

"I won't say anything if you don't," I said. "Tell them what I did, but leave Crawford out if it. Just tell me which way they went—quick."

"Left, a minute or so ago, maybe less." He pointed.

"Thanks, Claude, sorry."

And I was off. My Crosley was no match for the Ford, but Anthony might not be in a big hurry, might not want to get stopped by a cop and didn't know I was following him. I sped up looking for the Ford, passing through narrow spaces in the traffic, skidding along the curb at one point to pass an oversized Oldsmobile.

Then I saw the green Ford. I slowed down, staying three cars behind. He had seen my Crosley before, and there weren't many like it around.

We hadn't gone more than four or five blocks when the Ford made a sharp right turn into the parking lot of a restaurant called Hickory Heaven. There were no other cars in the lot, and there was a big sign on the side of the fake log-cabin exterior making it clear that the place was "Closed Temporarily for Renovation."

I drove past the parking lot, watching Anthony drive toward the door of Hickory Heaven. The next place I could turn right was the driveway of a gas station.

I pulled in and parked on the side of the pumps. Carrying my briefcase, I went inside the gas station, where a woman who looked like Marjorie Main stood behind the counter next to the cash register and looked at me.

"Call the police," I said. "Wilshire District. Ask for Detective Seidman. If he's not there, tell anyone that Toby Peters has Sheldon Minck at the Hickory Heaven restaurant and tell them where it is."

"What the hell did you just say?"

"I'll write it," I said, putting my briefcase down on the counter with a clunk and pulling out my notebook. I tried to balance the need for speed with the desire to be legible. I handed her what I had written, which included the phone number to call.

"You could have called yourself, the time it took you to tell me and write it down," she said.

"Right," I agreed, picking up the briefcase. "Just call. Life and death."

I ran out of the station, glancing back to see her pick up the phone while she shook her head and looked at the sheet of paper I had given her.

There was a fence between the gas station and Hickory Heaven. I was in no condition for climbing. I went to the sidewalk, made the turn, and quick-stepped to the parking lot. Briefcase open, I headed for the Ford. I could see it was empty. So, I went to the restaurant door and turned the handle. It was open. I went in.

There were no lights on but there were enough dust-dancing beams coming through the windows to see past the reception podium in front of me into the restaurant. Most of the tables and chairs were piled in a corner at the back. One table sat in the middle of the room. Behind it, facing me, sat Anthony and Joan Crawford. Anthony had a gun in his hand.

"Will someone please tell me what is happening?" Crawford asked.

"Be quiet and you'll find out," said Anthony, his eyes and gun on me.

"You expected me," I said, moving toward the table slowly.

"Saw you following in that little fridge of yours," he said. "Thought it best to get things done as soon as possible. I knew about this place and . . . by the way, when they reopen, if you are alive, you should definitely try their ribs and mashed potatoes with the house salad and a glass of their Napa cabernet."

"Spoken like a true Survivor," I said.

"I was not always as you see me now," he said with a smile.

"I gather from this that this man is not a policeman," said Crawford.

"He's not a policeman," I confirmed.

"No," said Anthony. "I'm a man with a simple mission. Peters, you are both to accompany me to the nearest telephone being very, very careful. There we will call Dr. Minck, who is safely watched and waiting. You will get from him the location of the will he wrote in the hotel."

"Or?"

"I'll put a bullet in the head of Miss Crawford," he said with a smile glancing at her. "And then another in you."

Crawford's face went pale.

"And if I get the information from Shelly, you let us go, kill him, and no hard feelings?"

"Haven't thought that part through yet," he said. "But we really don't need any more bodies cluttering the landscape. It's money we seek, not mayhem. I'm afraid you're right about Dr. Minck, though. He'll have to go. Can't have him writing more wills and can't collect if he's alive. That part's not negotiable. I'll make it as quick and painless as I can. Besides, with Minck no longer among the living, we won't care if Miss Crawford persists in saying she saw him kill his wife."

He was lying. After what he had just done and said, there was no way he could let Crawford and me live.

I considered my options. Go for the Buntline and risk getting Crawford shot, or stall and hope that the woman in the gas station had gotten through to someone who believed her.

"I've got to think about it," I said.

He looked at his wristwatch. "Not much to think about. Not much time to do it."

"What about Martha Helter?" I asked. "You were going to kill her in the hospital."

"Not necessary," he said. "Got enough from her to know she can't hurt us."

"You killed Lewis, sent her to the hospital, tried to kill me," I said.

"Is that a question?" he asked.

"People have a way of not surviving around and among the Survivors," I said. "All right if I sit?"

"Pull up a chair, but I'm afraid it will be a short rest. We have a phone call to make."

"Wait a minute," Crawford said. "I have something to say about this."

"I can't think what." Anthony gave her a pleasant smile.

"Suppose I won't go along with any of this," she said.

"Can't really see you have a choice," he said. "Peters?"

"You're Sax," I said, changing the subject while Crawford folded her arms and fumed.

"Not relevant," he said.

"Okay, let's try this one. We don't go along with what you want. You kill us. You have nothing."

"We still have Dr. Minck," he said. "And though he's proving difficult to persuade, we really haven't employed the most deplorable methods yet."

The door behind me to the restaurant shot open.

I pulled out the Buntline as Anthony stood and aimed over my shoulder. Before he or I could shoot, Crawford reached over, grabbed his hair, and scratched his face.

"Drop the guns," a voice behind me said.

I dropped the Buntline on the table, but Anthony pushed Crawford away and sent her tumbling over her chair onto the floor.

Blood trailing down his cheek, he aimed at Crawford. Bullets shot past me. I heard them, but none hit me. Anthony was blown back, his gun flying in the air. He didn't scream, just let out an "oooff" sound like an out-of-shape heavyweight taking a solid right to the midsection.

A uniformed cop ran past me. A second cop faced me, gun in hand.

"What's going on here?" asked the first cop, an old-timer with his hat tilted back.

I moved to help Crawford up. She gave me her hand. She looked dazed.

"My name's Peters," I said. "The lady is Billie Cassin."

Crawford was on her feet now.

"And I still don't know what's going on." the old-timer said, moving to the fallen Anthony. "We got a call on the radio. Said get over here and find Peters and Minck."

"You found one of them," I said.

"And a hell of a lot more," said the old-timer. "This guy's dead. Who is he?"

"He said his name was 'Anthony.' I think he might also be James Fenimore Sax. Cawelti at the Wilshire will fill you in."

"And that?" the cop asked, pointing at the Buntline with his pistol.

"An antique," I said. "Family heirloom. I'm a private investigator. I've got a permit to carry a gun."

I started to reach into my jacket. The second cop pushed my hand away and did the reaching. He came out with my wallet and found my card.

"He's a private investigator," he said. "Like he says."

"Go to the gas station next door," I said. "The woman there will tell you I was the one who told her to call the police."

"So," the old-timer asked again. "Kindly tell me who the hell I just killed. I haven't put a bullet through anyone since Verdun."

"He . . . it's a long story," I said.

"Best told to a detective," he said.

Crawford looked at me with large, pleading eyes.

"You happen to know Lieutenant Phil Pevsner?" I asked.

"Yeah," the old-timer said warily.

"He's my brother. He's at County Hospital. You can reach him through the nursing station on the sixth floor. He's on a case."

"He knows all about this?" asked the cop.

"Give him a call," I said.

The old-timer nodded to the younger cop watching me, and the younger cop put his gun away and headed for the pay phone next to the door.

"Can I get you a drink of water or something, Miss . . . ?"

"Cassin," she said, sitting at the table again. "No, thank you."

"You look a lot like—" the cop said, as I jumped in.

"Faint," I said.

The cop turned to me. "What?"

"The lady looks like she's going to faint," I said, raising my voice.

On cue, Crawford closed her eyes and conveniently dropped her arms and head on the table.

"I'll go in the kitchen and get her some water," I said not knowing if the water was turned on.

"All right, all right," said the cop, touching Crawford's shoulder. "Hurry up."

When I came back with the water, the younger cop was just getting back.

"Lieutenant Pevsner says we should wait right here," he said. "He's on the way. Said not to report this until he arrives, is what he said. And don't question either of these two."

While I gave Crawford some water, she winked at me without cracking a smile and the younger cop added, "Ted, you sure he's dead?"

"It's the coroner we're going to call, not an ambulance," said the older cop. "When the lieutenant gets here. Go to the gas

214

station next door and see if there's a woman there who'll confirm what Peters here says."

The young cop hurried away and the three of us who were still alive in the room sat down to wait. I thought I smelled the faint aroma of barbecue. It smelled good, but I didn't think I'd be taking Anthony's advice about returning to Hickory Heaven when it reopened.

CHAPTER

18

WATCHING PHIL WORK John Cawelti was the highlight of my year. Of course the year was just a little over a week old but I was sorely in need of a highlight.

We sat in the interrogation room at the Wilshire Station. Neither Cawelti nor Phil wanted to go into Phil's office. The two of them faced each other across the small table. I sat in the corner, a fly on the wall, a speck in the dust, a private eye watching silently. I was a catalog of near-biblical anonymity.

Cawelti began the battle with a careful attack. He knew Phil's flash-point anger, had seen my brother's fists drive hard, his face red with uncontrolled anger. Phil usually reserved his anger for criminals and his kid brother, but Cawelti was definitely catching him on a bad day.

"What are you doing, Phil?" Cawelti asked evenly.

"Looking across the table at a putz," Phil answered, just as evenly.

"Come on," Cawelti said. "We've got a problem here, a couple of dead people, one shot by a cop, a woman in the hospital, and a fugitive dentist."

"You've got a problem," Phil said. "Not 'we,' 'you.' I'm officially retiring."

"Effective in two weeks, DeVilbus tells me," Cawelti said.

"I'm touched," said Phil. "You're sorry to see me go."

Cawelti hesitated, thought, face starting to turn red.

"Truth? I'm not sorry to see you go," he said. "You know it. I know it. You don't like me. I don't like you and your smart-ass brother over there."

I smiled politely.

"You know my wife died," Phil said, looking at his fingernails, which I knew from experience was a dangerous sign.

"I know," said Cawelti carefully. "I'm sorry. Believe me."

"I don't think you give a shit either way," said Phil. "I was called to the scene of a crime. I wrote a report calling it justifiable homicide by the policeman on duty, Ted Havlichek. In fact, I'm recommending him for a departmental commendation. He saved the lives of two people from a nut with a gun."

"The nut with the gun was one of the Survivors for the Future, the group of nuts Minck is involved with," said Cawelti.

"He kidnapped the witness to Minck's killing his wife," Phil said.

"Why?" asked Cawelti. "I'll tell you. To make her take back her statement or to kill her. No witness, and maybe Minck walks."

"Could be," said Phil. "You've got signed statements from Toby, the woman. . . . "

Cawelti looked down at the papers in front of him and said, "Lucille LeSueur? I thought Crawford was using the name 'Billie Cassin.'"

"Lucille LeSueur is her real name," I said. "Billie Cassin is the stage name she used when she was a kid."

Cawelti patted the small stack of statements and reports in front of him.

"What you were doing at County Hospital?" he asked my brother, letting a small touch of aggression creep into his voice.

"Guarding your witness," Phil said. "I have good reason to believe Anthony—"

"Anthony Mastero," Cawelti supplied.

"Anthony Mastero"—Phil went on—"had made an attempt on Martha Helter's life while she was in the hospital."

"Why?"

"To keep her from telling where Sheldon Minck is," Phil said impatiently.

"Did she tell you?"

"No," said Phil. "She woke up a couple of times, talked a little, didn't know. You've got one more question. Then we're walking—after I pick up my things."

Cawelti tried to come up with something, but stalled.

"What do you have on Mastero?" I asked from my seat against the wall.

Phil looked over his shoulder at me. I think he was deciding who he was going to beat into the wall, me, Cawelti, or both of us. He had told me to be quiet. With more than forty years of experience with me, he should have known better.

Cawelti looked at me, then at Phil who nodded at him. Cawelti pulled a sheet from the bottom of the pile in front of him.

"Anthony Mastero, forty-two, Australian. Served time in Kansas for a jewelry-store robbery. Seven arrests, all for weapons-related charges. No convictions on those. California driver's license. Appendix scar, no military-service rec—"

"Aliases?" I interrupted.

Cawelti scanned the sheet.

"Tony McGuin, Terry Magnus, Thomas Meehan . . . Kept his initials."

"No Sax?" I asked.

Cawelti ran his finger down the page and said, "No, no Sax. Why?"

"We're leaving." Phil stood up. "John, I'd appreciate it if you'd put my things in a box and bring them to me in the hall."

I knew they were already in an orange crate. I got up and said nothing.

Cawelti was considering whether to say more and decided not to. He nodded and went into the hall. Phil and I followed.

We didn't talk. I knew Phil didn't want to face the awkward contact with the cops in the squad room. He had decided. That was it. Maybe later he would agree to a beer with a few of the people he had worked with, but right now all he wanted was to be gone and maybe someone to take a little more frustration out on.

Cawelti got Phil's things and brought them to us in the hall without a word. We left quietly.

"What now?" I asked when we were standing next to the rear of his car with the trunk open.

He put the box in and closed the trunk lid gently.

"You tell me," he asked.

"We find Shelly," I said.

"If he's still alive."

"If he's still alive," I echoed.

"Call me when you know, Tobias," Phil said. "I'm going home."

I waved as he got in his car and drove away.

I turned on the radio. The Chicago Bears and quarterback Sid Luckman had beaten the Washington Redskins and quarterback Sammy Baugh 41–21 for the world championship. Luckman had thrown five touchdown passes. Baugh had left the game early after tackling Luckman. A guy in a commercial told me that there was a good five-cent cigar, a Wedgewood panatela. He warned me that, because of the war, there was a limited output. If I found Shelly alive, I'd consider buying him a handful of panatelas.

Fifteen minutes later, I was back at my office in the Farraday with my briefcase and the Buntline of the late Mr. Plaut inside it.

The hour was late, but not so late the building didn't ring, rattle, and hum with voices and some things that might have been music.

There wasn't much to do except sit at my desk and wait for the phone to ring, hoping it was Shelly or whoever had survived of the Survivors and now had him. I also planned to call Mrs. Plaut's every hour to see if I got a call there.

Violet wasn't in. There was no reason for her to be. The lights were off. I unlocked the door and made my way to my office, turned on the light and checked the spindle on which Violet usually left me messages. The spindle was empty. I started to put both hands behind my head and got a sharp reminder of my still-sore shoulder and arm.

I sat and thought of what I might do next. Nothing came. After about twenty minutes of reading old mail, tearing it up, and dropping it in my wastebasket, I heard someone in the outer office. I looked up and Jeremy Butler filled the doorway.

"I saw your lights," he said. "Anything about Sheldon?"

"Not yet. Have a seat."

Jeremy sat.

"Is there anything I can do to help?" he asked.

"Not unless you tell me how to find James Fenimore Sax," I said.

"J. F. Sax," Jeremy repeated. "I can do that."

I think I took about ten seconds before I spoke and when I did it was slow and cautious.

"You can tell me where to find a J. F. Sax?"

"Yes," he said. "I believe the whole name is James Fenimore Sax."

"Where is he?" I asked.

"Two doors down. Professor Geiger's real name is James Fenimore Sax. He calls himself 'Professor Geiger,' but he signs his rent checks J. F. Sax or, if I remember correctly, when he first moved in, he signed them 'James Fenimore Sax.' Yes, I think I mentioned his name to him and told him of my fondness for some of James Fenimore Cooper's. . . ."

I was standing up and reaching for my briefcase.

"Come on," I said, hurrying around my desk and going to the door.

Jeremy rose and followed me.

"Is Geiger in?" I asked as we stepped through the outer door of Shelly's office.

"I don't know," Jeremy said. "I haven't heard that odd some-what haunting music from his Aeolian trafingle today."

"Martha Helter heard music on the phone," I said aloud, though I was talking to myself. "Funny music."

"Martha Helter?"

"Professor Geiger has Shelly," I said, walking down the hall with Jeremy at my side.

"Why?" Jeremy asked.

"Let's ask him." I tried the door to Geiger's office.

It was locked. There were no lights on inside.

"Do you know where he lives?" I asked Jeremy.

"Yes," he said. "I have his address upstairs in the office."

I had choices. I could bring Jeremy with me. I could call my brother. I could call Cawelti. I could even call Sax. Jeremy had given me his number. I didn't call anyone. I explained everything to Jeremy and told him what I was going to do. He wanted to come with me. I told him it would probably be better if no one was with me when I approached the house, and I asked him to call the police if he didn't hear from me in two hours.

He agreed reluctantly.

I don't know the real reason I wanted to go alone. It just felt like the right thing to do. Besides, I had the mister's Buntline in my briefcase.

The house was on Herbert Street just off Washington, a modest one-story stucco. Neat little front yard with an orange tree and a pair of palms about fifteen feet tall. The house looked pretty much like the other houses on the block.

I parked right in front. There were no people on the sidewalk and only a few cars in the driveways. If Sax was at the window, he would see me coming. What he wouldn't see was the Buntline I pulled out of the briefcase when I was right in front of the door. I placed the briefcase on the welcome mat and rang the bell.

James Fenimore Sax, alias Professor Alan Geiger, answered the door. In dark trousers and an open-necked white shirt with his Larry Fine hair brushed flat, he looked at me and the long revolver and stepped back to let me in.

"I gather you know," he said.

"Most of it," I said, walking in, gun pointing around the hallway and into the open living room where an Aeolian trafingle stood in the middle of the room among a clutter of furniture. The walls were racked with weapons: knives, bows, small guns, large rifles, even something that looked like a sling. In the middle of one wall was a large picture of Mark Twain. Twain had a target ring around his face. There were holes in the ring.

Sax saw me looking.

"Twain wrote a very spiteful and vindictive essay on James Fenimore Cooper," Sax said, walking ahead of me. "It ultimately ruined Cooper's critical reputation."

"Un-American," I said. "Where's Shelly?"

"In the other room, handcuffed to a metal bed," he said. "I'm glad you came. Shall we sit?"

"No, get Shelly," I said.

"Sorry. Sheldon tells me where he hid that will, and then we negotiate."

He removed three books from a chair and sat, crossing his knees and folding his hands.

"I'm the one with the big gun," I said.

"And I'm the one who has Joan Crawford."

"You do?"

222

"One of my men picked her up at Warner Brothers a few hours ago. I'm expecting a call from him any moment to ask me what to do with her. What should I have him do with her, Mr. Peters?"

He was smiling, picturing me, Shelly, and probably Joan Crawford dead.

"Shoot her dead."

He stopped smiling.

"Get Shelly," I repeated. "Anthony is dead. A cop shot him. Crawford is home."

"Bluff," said Sax. "If I don't answer the phone when Anthony—"

"He's dead," I repeated. "Shot full of holes. You've got to listen more carefully."

I could tell that he was beginning to believe me by the way his eyes went back and forth as if he were searching for a plan, the right line, a good idea.

"Get Shelly," I said.

"You won't kill me."

"Probably not, but I'm all for making a hole in your knee," I said. "I mean, *if* I shoot straight. I'm warning you. I don't shoot straight, and I have no idea what kind of damage a Buntline Special can do."

"We can deal," he said, nervous now.

"With what?"

"Minck *did* kill his wife," he said. "Hawkeye Anthony and I were in the bushes along the path in Lincoln Park. It went down all wrong. I had made a deal with Mildred Minck, given her the gun."

"You knew about the no-snore offer," I said.

"When Minck had joined the Survivors, he told me about the device and his patent. Among other things, I had Anthony check on it and discovered that the firm in Des Moines was interested. I called them pretending to represent Sheldon and found that they indeed were going to make a substantial offer."

"So you went to Mildred."

"I persuaded her to come to the park, told her where her husband would be. It shouldn't have been a problem. She could just shoot him and walk away a rich woman. I told her to be sure no one was watching when she did it."

"You were going to blackmail Mildred," I said.

"We had a camera," said Sax. "Anthony is . . . *was* very good with a camera."

"But Joan Crawford showed up," I said.

"Mildred was just pulling out her gun when Sheldon fired," said Sax. "Complete accident. Dumb luck. He had no idea he had shot her seconds before she was going to kill him. We didn't know what Crawford had seen. Anthony was going to go after Crawford, but he was too late. And then the kid came on the bicycle."

I waited while he paused and sighed.

"I improvised," he said. "Planted the second bolt after we saw the boy take the gun and the money. I wanted to suggest that Sheldon had missed the target and someone else had fired the bolt that killed Mildred. Actually, when we had left the scene, I decided that the mistake might be a good thing. Mildred's money would go to Sheldon, providing he wasn't convicted of killing her. Then, if I could get him out of jail and he had an accident, both of their considerable estates would go to me."

"So you could do a lot better than just blackmail Mildred," I said. "Life on a tropical island after the war."

"No," Sax said. "You've misjudged me. I believe in the Survivors."

"Which is why you get them killed?"

"I believe in them in a greater sense. Survival of the best, the committed. With money I can recruit more, grow, teach the frontier skills put forward, though not always with perfect accuracy, I admit, by my namesake."

"With you in charge," I said.

"I'm the founder. I'm James Fenimore, the creator of the movement."

"Creator?" I said. "A little god?"

"No."

"Okay, a Schickelgruber."

"Hitler's a monster," he said indignantly. "I'm a savior. There have to be sacrifices for the greater good."

"Open the door and get Shelly."

"I'll testify against him," Sax warned. "I'll confirm Crawford's story, say I had just arrived in time to see him shoot down the innocent woman who was almost certainly coming to reconcile with him."

I shot at the wall. The Buntline kicked me back about two feet. My left shoulder blazed with pain. The sound was an explosion, and I heard Shelly yelp from behind the thick, closed door to my left.

Sax was covering his head with both hands.

"I was aiming at you," I said, re-centering the Buntline at him. I should have been holding it in both hands, but my left arm had no intention of cooperating.

"You're crazy," Sax cried.

"Probably," I said. "I've had a bad week."

Sax got up and hurried to the closed door. He opened it with a key and I followed him in. Shelly, face puffed and purple, eyes almost closed, shirt bloody, sat on the floor chained to a metal bedpost.

"Toby," he said through swollen lips.

I think he tried to smile.

"The cuffs," I said to Sax, who moved to the bed and took the cuffs off Shelly, who said, "You got a cigar?"

"I'll get you one." Then to Sax: "Help him up."

Sax helped Shelly to his feet. Shelly wobbled unsteadily.

"Look what they did to you and you didn't talk, Shel," I said. "I'm proud of you."

"*Couldn't* talk," Shelly said.

"Why?"

"Didn't write that will," he said. "He'd kill me if I told him."

Sax's mouth dropped open. "I could have simply killed you."

Shelly did something that I think might have been a smile. Then he hauled back with his right hand and landed a nose-breaking punch in the middle of Sax's face.

"Survive that," Shelly said.

CHAPTER
19

Four days later, Professor Geiger's office was cleared out. Everything, including the Aeolian trafingle, was put in boxes and stored by Jeremy in a shed in the catacombs of the Farraday Building. There wasn't much chance that James Fenimore Sax was ever going to claim them, but Jeremy was taking no chances.

Sax made a deal with the district attorney. He signed a statement saying that he had been responsible for Mildred's going to the park to kill Shelly. The statement also said that he was positive Shelly had shot his wife accidentally.

In exchange, Sax was allowed to plead as an accessory to conspiracy to commit murder and to kidnapping. Anthony, he said, had planted the bomb that killed Lewis and sent Martha Helter to the hospital. Sax insisted it wasn't his idea to kill anyone but Shelly, and Shelly hadn't been killed. There would be no trial, no need for Joan Crawford's testimony. Sax would serve a minimum of twenty years without possibility of parole. Quick calculation made him close to eighty when he'd be eligible to get out.

It was early morning, before the tenants had begun climbing the stairs and moving slowly up the elevator to their offices.

Phil, Violet, Shelly and I stood outside the door and watched Jeremy scrape away the words "Professor Alan Geiger, Center for the Aeolian Trafingle" and carefully paint in plain black letters, "Pevsner and Peters, Confidential Investigations."

Shelly looked as if he were about to cry. He touched his face with the cast on his right hand. He had broken his fist with his right hook to Sax's face.

"We're only two doors down, Shel," I said.

"Yeah, but it's . . . it's different," he said.

"Shelly, you're a rich man now. You should be happy. You can buy all the latest dentist stuff," I said. "You don't even have to work if you don't want to."

"It's my calling," Shelly said.

Violet held his arm. Phil said nothing, just watched.

When he had finished the lettering, Jeremy opened the door and handed a key to me and another one to Phil. I could smell the fresh paint on the white walls. The office was a single room, no little reception/waiting area. The office was as big as Shelly's chamber. There was a closet on the wall to the left. Jeremy had gone into his trove of furniture and come up with two heavy dark wooden desks with almost-matching wooden swivel chairs behind them. There were two chairs in front of each desk and a phone on each. There was also a round wood table to the left with four chairs around it. On the table was a large vase full of flowers, big ones, red, yellow, pink, purple, with an envelope propped against the vase.

"That one's mine," said Phil, nodding at the desk to our right.

"Fine," I said moving to the table, picking up the envelope and opening it. There was a check inside for three hundred dollars signed by Joan Crawford. There was also a handwritten note:

> Good luck and sincere thanks. Should *Mildred Pierce* prove as successful for my career as I pray it will, it will, in no small way, be due to your efforts.
>
> J. C.

I put the note back in the envelope with the check. Later we would open an account at the bank for Pevsner and Peters with the three hundred dollars from me and the same amount from Phil.

The wall behind my desk was big enough for my Salvador Dalí painting of the mother and two babies in addition to the photograph of me, Phil, our dad and our dog Kaiser Wilhelm. I'd put them up later.

Jeremy had agreed to our paying the same rent I had been paying Shelly for my closet, with the understanding that if and when we could afford it, the rent would go up.

"But not significantly," Jeremy had assured us.

We all stood there for a few seconds, and then Phil moved to the window and looked down. I knew he was seeing the alley and small empty lot behind the Farraday.

"It's great, Jeremy, thanks," I said.

Phil nodded in agreement, turning from the window and looking around the room. His world had changed. I think with Ruth gone, that's what he wanted. I didn't know how we would work together—or *if* we could work together. We would see.

We stood silently, not knowing what to say.

The phone on Phil's desk rang. He picked it up, hesitated and said, "Pevsner and Peters," and then, "Yes. Right." He took his notebook, the same one he had been using as a cop, put it on the desk and pulled out a pencil. "Yes," he continued writing. "I've got it. We can get there in . . ."

Phil looked at his watch and then at me.

I put out both hands palms up to indicate that it was up to him.

" . . . about an hour," Phil finished.

He hung up the phone, looked down at his notebook and said, "Harry Blackstone wants to see us."

"The magician?" Violet asked excitedly. "The one who makes the lightbulb fly around the audience?"

"Yes," said Phil.

My brother and I looked at each other.

We were in business.